Steven Paulsen is an award-winning writer whose speculative fiction has appeared in publications around the world. His bestselling dark fantasy children's book, *The Stray Cat*, illustrated by Hugo and Oscar Award winning artist Shaun Tan, has seen publication in several English and foreign language editions. His short stories, which Jack Dann describes as rocket-fueled with narrative drive, have appeared in a variety of magazines and in anthologies such as *Terror Australis*, *Strange Fruit*, *Cthulhu: Deep Down Under*, *Fantastic Worlds*, *The Cthulhu Cycle*, and the World Fantasy Award winning *Dreaming Down-Under*.

Steven has also written extensively about Australian horror and fantasy for publications such as Eidolon, Interzone, Bloodsongs, Sirius, The Encyclopedia of Fantasy, Fantasy Annual, The St James Guide to Horror, Ghost and Gothic Writers, and The Melbourne University Press Encyclopaedia of Australian Science Fiction and Fantasy. His interviews with Australian SF writers have been published in magazine and book form in Australia, UK, Europe and the USA.

Readers can find out more about Steven's work at:
www.stevenpaulsen.com

T0165057

Praise for *Shadows on the Wall*

"No matter the genre, there's a dark undercurrent in Paulsen's work, a gleeful malevolence that betrays a deeply nihilistic worldview somehow both addictive and soul-shattering."
  - Aaron Sterns, author *Wolf Creek: Origin*, co-writer *Wolf Creek 2*

"Paulsen's body of work, as evidence by this impressive collection, explores the nature of our fears, effortlessly exposing us to shuddering horrors and milder terrors while drawing us in with utterly real characters."
  - Kaaron Warren, author *The Grief Hole*

"Paulsen's tales range across the past, present and future, from settings totally common to the exotic and the magical. Uniting these wide-ranging tales is an unsettling, often supernatural, essence that puts his characters -- and his readers' perceptions of reality -- to the test."
  - Jason Nahrung

"From its fathomless Lovecraftian horrors to the more intimate terrors that dwell far too close to home, this career-spanning collection deserves a prominent place in any library of quality Australian dark fiction."
  - Kirstyn McDermott

"The beauty of Steve Paulsen's Shadows on the Wall lies in its accessibility: dark though the stories may be, we read them and nod - we know. Off the wall though its characters may be, they live next door. Reading Shadows is like talking to the neighbours - if you do (if you dare) you might just learn something about life."
  - Gary Crew, Author of *Strange Objects*

"Shadows on the Wall will take you into some dangerously dark places, places that you know you should not enter, but enter you will, for, alas, you won't be able to help yourself. The stories contained within are rocket-fueled with narrative drive. These subtle, ironic, humorous, and sometimes horrific extrapolations and fantasies showcase Paulsen's wild talent and tight grip on craft."

   - Jack Dann

"Don't let the domestic settings fool you - these stories confront the murky truths that lurk deep in the hidden heart of humanity. Paulsen peers over the brink of the abyss - and sees dark Lovecraftian forces looking right back at him. This collection is strong stuff - read it at your own risk."

   - Janeen Webb

Shadows on the WALL

Weird Tales of Science Fiction, Fantasy, and the Supernatural

By Steven Paulsen

Shadows on the Wall

All Rights Reserved

ISBN-13: 978-1-925496-57-4

V1.0 US

Publishing history at end of this book. Frontispiece by Shaun Tan.

Printed in Palatino Linotype, Courier New and Signo.

IFWG Publishing International
Melbourne
www.ifwgaustralia.com

To Edward, Laura and Sarah
and to my dad, Allan

and in loving memory of Anne
and my mum, Lois

Acknowledgements

Thank you to IFWG Publishing Australia and Gerry Huntman; to Shaun Tan; to Isobelle Carmody; to Jack Dann; to the editors who originally published many of these works; to the artists who illustrated them, and to all the people who have supported my writing over years: Justin Ackroyd, Neville Angove, Leigh Blackmore, Simon Brown, Jeremy G. Byrne, Helen Chamberlin, Paul Collins, John Robert Colombo, Bill Congreve, David Conyers, Gary Crew, Kirstyn McDermott, Terry Dowling, Kathryn Duncan, Michal Dutkiewicz, Geoff Ebbs, Sarah Endacott, Peter Enfantino, Russell Farr, Rebecca Fraser, Micheal Graham, Philip Harbottle, Richard Harland, Stephen Higgins, Rob Hood, Van Ikin, Rick Kennett, Keira McKenzie, Simone Knight, Geoff Maloney, Chris A. Masters, Sean McMullen, Jason Nahrung, Peter McNamara, Garth Nix, Robin Pen, Robert M. Price, Stephen Proposch, Barry Radburn, David Riley, John Scoleri, Richard Scriven, Christopher Sequeira, Jonathan J Sequeira, Deborah Sheldon, Bryce J. Stevens, Kurt Stone, Jonathan Strahan, Dirk Strasser, Chris Stronach, Stephen Studach, Lucy Sussex, Paul Voermans, Sean Wallace, Kaaron Warren, Daniel Watson, Janeen Webb, Sean Williams and Maurice Xanthos.

Table of Contents

Foreword

Isobelle Carmody

There is a yearning in humans that fascinates me. A spark that rises up. A longing for radiance, for beauty, maybe even for goodness.

But there is a Void in our kind, too. It frightens me. I don't want to look into it. But to ignore it would be to lie to myself about what we are. We need to be aware of this inner Void, this emptiness that can so easily fill with despair and terror and unspeakable acts of cruelty and violence. The Void speaks to us of that capacity. But to look into it requires courage because most often, it is our own faces that will look back at us.

These stories from Steve Paulsen capture that awful recognition because despite ranging far from one another in terrain, they all conjure startlingly real and visceral glimpses of the Void. They externalise it. They force us to experience it. They make us question our perceptions, our beliefs, wonder what we would be truly capable of if the chips were down. Some of the stories allow us to master the Void. In others, the Void looks back and in others, the Void consumes us.

Their particular potency lies in the honed sharpness of the writing, in the repertoire of emotional responses to strangeness they offer through brilliant and detailed characterisation. From the ominous hungers of 'The Place', to the lovely yearning sadness counterpointed by the horrific potential in 'Two Tomorrow', the characters in these stories are real enough to show us to ourselves. Sometimes this is reassuring, sometimes confronting, and sometimes threatening. We soon learn that nothing can be trusted. Certainly not our sensibilities.

Even when the setting is exotic, such as in 'Ma Rung', it is less the beautifully drawn Vietnamese jungle in war time that strikes us, than the recognisable humanity of the Australian soldiers moving through it. The considerable strength of this story lies in the juxtaposition of the rough familiarity of men we might know and the terrible alien-ness of war; the story hinging not on the obviousness of violence, but on the delicate strangeness of the Void, beautifully concluded with a quick disconcerting sidestep back to normality.

The setting is even more exotic in 'The Sorcerer's Looking Glass' because it presents as fantasy and openly draws on fairy tale tropes, yet it is the domestic that resolves the terror at the heart of the tale.

My favourites are the quirky 'Greater Garbo', and the marvellous 'Pest Control', both of which evoke the Void through the domestic, making it as horrifying as if we had looked into a plug hole to see an eye peering back at us. And with 'Old Wood', the uncanny is brought with the lightest of touches into a relationship, thereby suggesting all the grotesquely violent potential that can hide inside any relationship.

Counterpointing the rest is the retro adventure, 'The Black Diamond of the Elephant God', which is so meticulously detailed in its telling that we feel ourselves to be caught in the deadly undertow of the protagonist's fascination with the black diamond. As so often in all of the stories in this collection, the writing here is rich enough to allow wonderfully transcendent ambiguities.

"Do you believe in God?" asks the Brahmin priest Shankar.

"Sometimes," Giles answers.

These stories are beautifully written and subtle, and in their subtlety, they linger uneasily in the minds. They are shadows, shifting on the wall, barely seen, slipping into our minds to lie, light and cold over our hearts...

Isobelle Carmody
September 2017

Ma Rung

Take a man and put him alone,
Put him 5000 miles from home,
Empty his heart of all, but blood,
Make him live in sweat and mud.

— Anonymous Vietnam Digger,
'The Boys Up There'

'Long Green', East of Dat Do, Phuoc Tuy Province, Vietnam —
12 March, 1968.

Concealed in the jungle on a ridge above the Viet Cong mortar platoon, Sergeant Steve Lund gave the SAS patrol its instructions. He sent "Johnno" Johnson and Evans, the medic, around to the left of the enemy, while Papas and Barnes took the right flank. Lund stayed behind with Hutchinson, the signaller, to set up the M-60 bipod machine gun.

Clad in badgeless tiger-stripe uniforms, camouflage cream smeared on faces and arms, the men melted without a sound into the sun-dappled undergrowth. Jungle phantoms.

Taking up position within sight of the enemy, Johnson slid the water bottle from his belt, careful not to make a sound, and rinsed the dust from his dry mouth. Stinging sweat trickled into his eyes. He replaced the bottle and checked his rifle magazine, turning the weapon's safety catch to full automatic. Finally, he removed a white phosphorous grenade from his webbing and settled back to wait for the signal.

Insects buzzed and flitted in the hot air.

Suddenly, movement in the gully below the VC caught Johnson's attention. He swore under his breath as he recognised a patrol of hapless Diggers blundering into the enemy's line of sight.

Then there was activity from the VC—they too had seen the Australian infantrymen and were hastily repositioning their mortars.

Johnson levelled his rifle.

"Wait for the signal," hissed Evans as he took one of the white egg-shaped grenades from his own webbing and clicked it into the launcher at the end of his rifle.

There was a short series of hollow thuds from the Viet Cong position as the mortars began. Their first shells fell short, exploding in clouds of dirt, branches and other debris. But one found its mark, sending the Australian soldiers flying, shrapnel tearing through them.

Johnson gritted his teeth. He squinted with the sun in his eyes. Sweat ran in rivulets down his face, neck, and back.

Finally the signal, a burst of M-60 tracer, streamed into the VC camp. The white grenades followed from left and right, exploding with short, sharp cracks, spewing eruptions of deadly white phosphorous.

A screaming VC burst from cover, writhing, limbs flailing, the upper part of his body burning like a roman candle. But his agonised cries were cut short by a compassionate round from the M-60.

Other VC charged through the jungle towards Johnson's and Evans's position. Johnno brought his rifle to bear and spurted the full twenty-eight rounds from the magazine into the moving shrubs. A torrential rain of bullets ripped through the enemy from three points.

Then silence descended over the jungle once again.

Smoke drifted aimlessly amid the shredded foliage, the sickly-sweet smell of burnt flesh pervading the air. A lone bird began to chirp and chatter somewhere high in the trees.

Johnson slammed home a new magazine and moved cautiously forward, his rifle muzzle pointing wherever his eyes looked, his hand motioning Evans to fall in behind. Avoiding the paths and tracks, they moved swiftly and silently through the jungle, down into the gully, leaving the others to mop up any remaining pockets of VC resistance. Cries from the wounded Diggers penetrated the dense greenery and led them towards the fallen patrol.

Parting a fan of jungle fronds, Johnson revealed the clearing in which the Aussies had fallen. They lay scattered near the centre, two black-clad VC guerrillas standing over them with bloodied knives drawn.

Outrage and fury welled up and made Johnson's chest go tight. Even as he watched, the closest of the guerrillas turned his attention to a wounded Digger desperately trying to squirm to safety. Johnson yanked back hard on the trigger of his rifle and sprayed the VC, his bullets spinning the men around, shredding their chests like butcher's meat.

Entering the clearing, Johnson and Evans hurried to the aid of the two Australians still alive. Evans knelt by a corporal with most of his lower jaw missing—the man was gasping for breath, red bubbles forming and bursting in the cavity, his face splashed with blood and saliva. Johnson went to the other man, the one who had been trying to squirm away. This soldier had been hit in both legs, but appeared otherwise unharmed.

"It hurts like fuck," the man gasped as his gaze fell on the SAS corporal.

"Easy, mate." Johnson quickly jabbed him with a shot of morphine, tore a field dressing open with his teeth, and began to tend to his legs.

"The bastard was gonna kill me!"

"Take it easy, mate—dustoff choppers'll be here soon. Before you know it, you'll…"

Johnson's head jerked up, his keen hearing had detected a sound; dry twigs or leaves crunching, the swish of foliage. He

5

motioned the wounded man to silence and raised his rifle.

Suddenly a half-naked, frightened-looking VC guerrilla, hardly more than a kid, burst into the clearing, his AK-47 barking and kicking as it spewed tracer.

The soldier Evans was tending bucked and jerked, blood and flesh spraying from him. Evans went down with a scream as his legs were shot out from under him.

Johnson swung his weapon at the gunman, squeezed the trigger, and threw himself to the ground. His rifle squirted a round, which went high, then jammed.

The VC triumphantly turned the muzzle of his gun towards Johnson, but for some reason did not fire. Instead, the man's mouth fell open and his eyes grew wide in terror.

"*Ma qui!*" the VC yelped, shaking his head, his eyes bulging. He lowered his rifle, and began to back away. "*Ma rung...*" It sounded like a plea for mercy.

Johnson cocked his rifle, checked the chamber with trembling fingers for a jammed case. Clear. But before he could adjust the regulator, two pistol shots rang out and the crazed VC guerrilla crumpled to the ground.

Johnson rolled over to see Steve Lund brandishing his automatic pistol, emerging from the jungle. Behind him came Hutchinson and the rest of the patrol.

"Check the VC for papers, diaries, maps," Lund snapped. "Papas, help Evans. Hutchinson, call in a dustoff chopper and get these blokes out of here." He turned to Johnson. "You all right, mate?"

Johnson clambered to his feet and shook his head slowly from side to side. "I thought I was a fuckin' goner." He threw his arm around Lund's shoulder and squeezed him. "Thanks, pal. You saved my life. Perfect timing, you scared the shit out of the nog. He had me, my rifle had a stoppage."

Lund shook his head. "It wasn't me who scared him, mate. I was still drawing my pistol when he stopped shooting. He saw something else, not me."

Johnson looked puzzled. "What'd he see?"

"Dunno. Shadows...Somethin'." Lund blew his breath out.

He lowered his voice. "Shit, Johnno, it looked like there were blokes standing over there."

"Blokes?"

"Those poor bastards behind you," Lund indicated the fallen Diggers. "I saw 'em...I saw somethin'. *He* saw 'em. That's what scared the little prick, not me."

"Don't be fuckin' stupid," Johnson said. "If the brass hear you talkin' like that you'll be hauled in front of the shrink before you can say Jack Robinson."

Lund studied his friend's face for a moment, then shrugged free of his arm. "C'mon Hutchinson," he yelled, "where's that flamin' chopper?"

I got a letter from me sheila the other day,
She said, "I've found a new bloke while you've been away,"
So I got pissed with me mates, Darryl and Fred,
Best mates I ever had, but now they're both dead.

— Rob Dawson, 'Me Mates'

SAS Hill, Task Force Headquarters, Nui Dat, Vietnam — 23 April, 1968.

"What the fuck are ya doin' out there?"

Steve Lund was sitting outside on a folding chair with his back to the tent, his feet soaking in an enamel dish of scarlet-purple water.

"Tryin' to get rid of this bloody tinea," Lund yelled. "Whadda ya reckon?"

"Huh?" Johnno Johnson emerged from the tent, only to shy away from the sunlight. "Jesus it's bright, dunno how ya can

7

stand it. What's that purple shit?"

"I can stand it, mate, because I stuck to Tiger beer when the Fosters ran out last night. You drank nearly a whole bottle of Bundy. That stuff'll kill ya."

"Bullshit, it puts hairs on your chest."

Lund was studying his feet. "This purple shit's Condy's crystals. Reckon it'll do any good?"

Johnson snorted. "Wouldn't count on it." He yawned and stretched, gazing bleary-eyed across the campsite, noticing men hanging around in small groups outside the tents and prefabs erected among the plantation rubber trees. "What's everyone doin' out there?"

"Same as me. Waitin' for Mouth Matthews."

"*Him*? Why bother?"

"'Cause the blokes over in Two Squadron got fed up with the little prick last night. They got him paralytic, walked him out to the urinals, made sure he fell into one of the drums full of piss, fished him out, chucked him in that tent over there and closed it up." Lund chuckled and looked up at the sun. "How hot do you reckon it is? Eighty? Ninety? By the time the dickhead wakes up, he'll be fuckin' ripe. I don't wanna miss it."

"Neither does half the camp," Johnson said, nodding at the men hanging around, smoking, chatting.

"What about you, Johnno? You okay today?"

"Whadda ya mean?"

"About Rhonda, droppin' ya."

"Yeah, bitch. She never could go without it for long."

"You can talk," guffawed Lund. "How many of those bar girls in Saigon and Vung Tau have you screwed?"

"That's different."

"Yeah, I know, you went on and on about it last night. Lucky I'm your mate. Nobody else would've put up with ya."

"Get stuffed." Johnson gave him two fingers. "Look at the shit I have to put up with from you."

"That's what mates are for. You can count on me, pal." He chuckled. "How about a beer? I reckon these Condy's crystals make a bloke thirsty."

Johnson disappeared into the tent and returned with two open cans of Tiger beer. "They're warm."

"Who cares as long as it's wet."

Johnson lobbed one to Lund who caught it with practised ease, holding it clear while some of the beer frothed over. "Hey, did ya hear what the nogs are callin' us?"

"Callin' who?"

"Us, the SAS."

"Nuh."

"*Ma Rung. Ma*-bloody-*rung.*"

"What's it mean?"

"Umm… Forest spirits. Tree men. Phantoms or ghosts of the jungle." Lund snorted. "Something like that. They reckon Ho Chi Minh's put a price on our head. Six thousand piastres."

"Cheap skate. We're worth a darn sight more than that. Ho Chi Minh's a cunt."

Both men laughed. Lund raised his can of beer in a toast. Johnson did the same. They touched cans, and gulped down the warm beer.

"Lundy…?"

Lund wiped his mouth with the back of his hand. "What?"

"*Ma Rung*… Isn't that what that crazy VC said? You know, in the clearing after the mortar attack?" Johnson took another gulp of beer. "When you saved my life. When you reckon you saw somethin'…?"

"I never saw anythin', mate. Shadows, that's all."

"Sure." Johnson nodded. "Whatever you say. I owe you for that, Lundy."

"Any time, pal. We're mates."

They clinked cans.

"Yeah, mates."

"You gonna hang around for Mouth Matthews?"

"Wouldn't miss it for quids."

The green banana grove, and the betel palm,
Seas of green rice, and plains of silver water,
All are home to the ghosts of the fallen,
Who tread the paths of lost souls.

— Tran Thanh, 'Ma Rung' (translated by
William Cobb)

Near Bien Hoa and Phuoc Tuy Province border, Vietnam — 9 October,
1968.

Johnson was in front on point, Hutchinson was bringing up the rear and the rest of the patrol were strung out in between. They were on a high priority reconnaissance mission into a free fire zone—here anything that moved was fair game.

During the previous half hour they had spent only ten minutes on the move, olive-drab shadows, and for the other twenty minutes they had remained as motionless as statues; listening, watching, dripping with perspiration.

It was pack-time—the time when enemy traffic was heaviest—and the SAS patrol was approaching a known North Vietnamese Army route.

Johnson gave the thumbs down signal and the six men sank into the lush undergrowth. Twelve feet from them, a North Vietnamese Army platoon was passing along an intersecting track.

They watched and counted and listened.

It was almost an hour later when eventually they moved on.

The SAS avoided tracks, instead they moved like stalking cats through the almost impenetrable walls of the jungle. When it was necessary to cross a track, they waited, listened, watched, then moved across it one by one at short intervals. Now, Johnno Johnson listened, straining hard for any sound unusual to the jungle. Birds twittered and chirped, insects buzzed. He moved…

The low-pitched bark of a Russian-made AK-47 assault rifle sent the SAS commandos diving for the spongy musty-smelling jungle floor.

Johnson staggered as the first burst of automatic fire ripped through his upper arm. The second shattered his left kneecap and he suppressed an agonised scream as his leg collapsed and he went down hard.

In reply, another burst of automatic fire tore through the thick jungle foliage, this time the higher trilling of Papas' American-made M-16. Before the last spent cartridge had hit the ground, the splintering crack of breaking branches sounded from the canopy and a khaki-clad North Vietnamese regular plummeted from a nearby tree, his jungle-leaf hat following after him.

The confrontation was over as quickly as it had begun.

Sergeant Lund appeared at Johnson's side with Evans, the medic. After a cursory examination, they swiftly administered a pain killer, lifted Johnno between them and slipped soundlessly back into the jungle. They travelled quickly and quietly for some distance before finally stopping to attend to his injuries.

"Jeez you're a lucky bastard, Johnno," Lund said in low tones. "Fuckin' hell, you should be dead by rights."

Johnson grimaced as Evans cleaned his shoulder wound. "Thanks for the vote of confidence," he said through gritted teeth.

Lund's tone became serious. "We've got a problem, mate. We're gonna have to push on." The sergeant frowned and rubbed his crew-cut stubble. "We can't take you with us, so we're gonna have to leave you here and pick you up on our way back tomorrow. Okay?"

Johnson nodded, "Yeah, I understand."

"I can leave a bloke with you if—"

"It's all right," interrupted Johnson. "I'll be okay. You need every man for the mission. And like you said, I'm bloody lucky."

They dug Johnson in beneath a tangle of thick undergrowth at the foot of an ancient forest tree. When he was comfortable they whispered farewells and Lund signalled the patrol to move out.

But as the sergeant made to follow his men, Johnson grabbed his sleeve, holding him back.

"Listen Lundy," Johnno said. "I want you to do something for me." He fiddled with the thin gold chain around his neck, trying to release the catch. "I want you to take this cross." It came loose and Johnson held it out to Lund, a small gold cross on a thin chain. "If for some reason I don't make it, I want you to make sure my mum gets this." He gave a humourless chuckle. "She gave it to me for luck."

"There's no need for this, mate. You'll be fine. All you gotta do is sit tight."

"Come on Lundy, humour me. Just in case."

"Okay, Johnno." Lund shook his head. "But you're taking a risk. What if I don't make it?"

"You better, pal. I'm relying on you."

The afternoon torrential rain started shortly after the others had left, as Johnson had known it would. It beat monotonously upon his jungle hat and drenched him to the skin within minutes. The worst part was, he knew it would fall at the same soaking rate until sometime during the night.

He was uncomfortable. Unlike his arm, which he couldn't even feel, his leg throbbed painfully. The painkillers Evans had administered were beginning to wear off, and what had started as a dull ache was now becoming difficult to bear. He contemplated the additional syringe the medic had left him, but decided to save it until the last possible moment.

He felt strangely vulnerable in his dugout refuge between the jutting roots of what looked like a giant rubber tree. Unusually so because not only was he hidden by the roots, he was also surrounded by thick undergrowth making him virtually invisible to the probing eye.

This exposed feeling nurtured a growing desire to act, to do something. But there was nothing he could do but wait. Wait for rendezvous with the others and, hopefully, safe extraction. Or wait, who knew how long, for the inevitable.

He checked his rifle: it was set to full automatic. He listened, straining hard for sounds beyond the relentless patter of large raindrops and the trickle of running water.

Already the jungle floor was underwater, transformed into a shallow swamp. Johnson felt like he was sitting in a tepid bath. But it was not refreshing. He was hot, starting to burn up with a growing fever.

He listened and waited, all the time his fever and pain increasing. He watched large blue-black flies edging their way towards his bloodied bandages. He thought about home, and wondered if he would ever return. Images of Rhonda came unbidden, her curly blonde hair, her large pale-nippled breasts. Strangely, he imagined himself standing in the outer at the MCG, watching the cricket. He remembered drinking Tarax creamy soda at the corner milk bar… It all seemed *so* far away.

The pain intruded and brought him back to the dank-smelling jungle. He wanted to moan, but was too scared someone would hear. He gritted his teeth and thought about Lund and the other blokes on the mission. Would they come back? Or would he be left to die there in the dirt and mulch of the jungle floor like some wounded animal? Lundy wouldn't leave him. Lundy was a mate. Johnno pressed his eyes closed, squeezing out a few tears, breathing heavily. He tried to make plans, think of a way out, until finally he could think of nothing else but his pain. It burned and throbbed through his entire body. Then he administered the morphine Evans had left him.

The agony subsided as the drug took effect and shortly he began to feel drowsy. Night approached and the rain continued monotonously and Johnson fell into an uneasy sleep. A sleep tormented by weird dreams and spasms of pain. Dreams in which Viet Cong soldiers were fucking Rhonda, where the patrol did not return and Johnno was forced to crawl through the jungle on shattered limbs.

Johnson awoke with a fright, startled by a ruckus in the trees above him. He swung his rifle clumsily toward the commotion with his good arm, realising as he did so that it was only a group of tiny monkeys, probably arguing over a piece of fruit.

It was morning. His lips were dry and his throat was parched. He took a drink from his water bottle and allowed himself a moment to reassess his situation while he woke fully.

The jungle was steaming, the rain had stopped now, and the morning sun was reclaiming the moisture. Johnson's shirt and kit had already dried out, but the hole in which he was sitting was still half full of muddy water and his trousers and boots were sodden.

His head was woozy and his wounds throbbed.

Gritting his teeth, Johnson lifted his injured leg from the hole and propped it against one of the tree roots. Despite his care the movement sent jagged shards of pain shooting up his leg and beads of sweat broke out on his forehead. He unsheathed his knife and cut the remains of his olive-drab jungle trousers off at the thigh. He bent over to examine his leg and cursed.

There were at least half a dozen bloated leeches stuck fast to his leg and there were sure to be others elsewhere. He felt his stomach muscles contract as he thought of the little buggers latching onto his balls. He wanted to take out his waterproof matches and fry the fat grey creatures until they curled up and dropped from his body. But even in his fevered state his training would not allow it. The smell of burning phosphorus might be enough to give him away. Instead, he checked his dressings and settled back to wait, trying to put the bloodsuckers out of his mind.

He hoped everything was going according to plan. The others should return sometime around midday, depending on enemy concentration. Not so long.

Enemy concentration.

Johnson peered out of his hidey-hole, searching the jungle, but he found it hard to focus. He drank some more water. His fevered mind began to conjure up weird paranoid scenarios. He imagined VC moving through the jungle, and at one stage he felt certain there was somebody hiding in the foliage above, watching him. Then he began to think the VC were waiting to spring a trap for Lundy and the others.

The pain in his leg began to throb in time with his heartbeat. Johnno felt light-headed and knew he was feverish. He removed the magazine from his rifle, examined it, and carefully clicked it home again, terrified the sound would be heard.

He started counting ants to calm himself, get control.

Then he heard movement: branches cracking, the swish of foliage as something brushed past. His first thought was that the others had returned, and only his training stopped him from calling out. Besides, they would not have made so much noise.

Johnno pulled himself with his good arm to a vantage point, but had to steady himself as his head spun and he felt faint. Then he heard voices, Vietnamese voices. Slowly parting the foliage before him, Johnson could see a group of North Vietnamese Army soldiers stopped in conversation on a nearby track.

One of them broke away from the others as he watched, striding purposefully towards Johnson's position. Johnson levelled his rifle, breaking into a cold sweat as the man continued to close the distance between them. Finally, just as Johnson began to tighten his finger on the trigger, the man stopped, barely a couple of yards from the muzzle of Johnno's rifle, and began to kick away a patch of underbrush.

Sweat dripped off the end of Johnson's nose. His heartbeat seemed so loud, he felt sure it would give him away. The soldier appeared to be looking straight at him and he found it an effort to resist the urge to fire.

Then the North Vietnamese soldier lowered his khaki trousers and squatted to relieve himself. Johnson silently let out the breath he had been holding, and noticed he was trembling.

But just at that moment when Johnno thought he was safe, the enemy soldier lurched wildly to his feet with his trousers around his ankles, and began yelling as he fumbled with his rifle.

Johnson squeezed the trigger, spraying the man with automatic fire at point blank range, making him dance convulsively and sending pieces of his equipment flying into the air.

Silence followed. The other North Vietnamese soldiers had disappeared. Johnson wriggled back into the cover of his dugout.

Suddenly the jungle exploded as AK-47 shells ripped through the shrubs and treetops, shredded foliage falling to the ground all around him. Then it stopped.

Johnson waited, listening; they were unsure of his exact position. He heard a rustle then a clunk over to his left—almost too late he realised it was a grenade and he crouched, crying out in pain, in the bottom of his hole. Nevertheless, the explosion that followed flung him backwards and stunned him.

Johnno shook his head, the only sound he could hear was a ringing inside his skull. Pieces of splintered tree trunk had punctured his face and arms like darts, and acrid smoke choked his lungs.

He blacked out.

As he began to come around, Johnson experienced a peculiar feeling. A sense of detachment, as though he were observing events rather than participating. He thought for a moment that he must be dead, then the quiet blackness gradually gave way to bright sunlight and the racket of a frenzied rifle exchange.

His head swam and his vision was blurred. Then he knew he must be alive, because his leg still burned and throbbed exactly as it had before the grenade had gone off. Looking around, half squinting into the morning sun, he could make out the silhouette of someone standing over him, someone madly firing a rifle into the jungle.

Not a moment too soon, Johnno thought. He shielded his eyes trying to focus. He felt certain it was his mate Steve Lund standing over him.

But Lund's silhouetted image seemed to fade and waver, like a picture on a poorly tuned TV. Once he thought it was Rhonda, then his mum. Johnson shook his head and rubbed his eyes. A rush of dizziness and nausea hit him and his vision blurred. Gradually the feeling passed and he looked up again.

He could still see the shadowy figure above him, oblivious to the North Vietnamese fire directed at them.

"Lundy?" Johnson's voice was a feeble croak.

"Keep your head down, mate," a voice came between bursts. It sounded like Lundy. The figure sprayed another round into the jungle.

"Lundy…"

Dizziness again. He broke out in a cold sweat.

Even though he could not make out his friend's face, Johnno felt certain Steve Lund was looking down, smiling. But Johnson sensed it was a sad, longing sort of smile.

"Careful, mate," Johnson managed as darkness overtook him once more. "I'm relying on you."

When Johnson next came around, he had the sensation of movement and realised the gunfire had ceased.

"Lundy…" he mumbled. "Lundy…"

"Sleepin' Beauty's awake," a voice said.

The movement stopped and Johnson opened his eyes. He was lying on the ground with Evans, the patrol medic, bent over him. By his feet, Hutchinson was on the radio.

"Safe extraction signal green," Hutchinson said. "Over."

Johnson could see the green smoke signal billowing into the air above them.

"Okay," said a metallic voice on the radio, "I see green. Out."

"Here, have a drink." Evans held an uncapped water bottle to Johnno's lips. "You've earned it—looks like you had quite a time with those nogs." Evans lifted Johnson's head so he could slurp groggily at the water. It trickled down his chin and neck. Then Evans lowered his head back to the ground and turned his attention to Johnno's wounds.

Johnson lifted his good hand to wipe away the spilled water, and his fingers came in contact with the gold cross around his neck. He smiled to himself, thinking Sergeant Lund must have replaced it while he had been unconscious.

Evans's voice interrupted Johnson's thoughts. "I can hear the chopper—we'll be out of here before you know it, Johnno." He offered him another drink.

"No," groaned Johnson. "Thanks." He rolled his head to look for Lund. "You guys showed up just in time. Where's the Sarge?"

Evans licked his lips and didn't meet his eye. "I'm afraid Lund didn't make it, Johnno. The poor bastard copped a VC booby trap last night. Jumpin' Jack. Blew 'im to fuckin' bits."

Johnson shook his head incredulously. It was impossible. Lundy had saved his life. He had *seen* him.

"I know it's a funny thing to say," Evans went on, "but I reckon you're lucky that sniper put you out of action. Otherwise it would have been you on point."

"No," Johnson croaked as the extraction helicopter appeared above them in a burst of noise and wind. "It's bullshit," he protested. "Lundy saved me." But his cries went unheard as the chopper descended noisily into the clearing, the grass around them rippling in the wash of its rotor blades. The air felt cool against the heat of Johnson's face.

Johnson's searching gaze darted about, confused, as they lifted him into the belly of the chopper. He couldn't see his mate. Lund *was* missing. Johnno clutched for the thin gold chain around his neck, found it and jerked it free. How could it be? He held his hand up in front of his face, but saw only a faint glimmer before his vision blurred and he was forced to close his eyes.

"Easy, Johnno," came Evans's soothing voice close to his ear. Fingers pried the chain from his grasp. "Careful, mate, or you'll lose that. Let me take it."

Johnson tried to speak, to yell his denial, his confusion, but his feeble whisper was drowned by the sound of the helicopter.

Darkness began to close in on him.

"I'll have you blokes safely back in a jiffy," Johnson heard the pilot yell as the machine lurched into the air.

Then he passed out.

Ma Rung — Afterword

Scenes of the Vietnam War were beamed into our lounge room on the six o'clock news every night when I was a teenager. Helicopters with thwacking rotor blades. Terrified children running from burning villages. Steaming jungles. Young men bearing weapons patrolling rice paddies.

At first it all seemed remote, until a mate's older brother proudly volunteered and was sent off to fight. A girl I was keen on fell in love with a "nasho", and he went AWOL and they ran away together. Then the kid across the road received his call-up papers. The Vietnam War was suddenly personal, looming over all our lives.

In this story, I wanted to reflect on those memories: the fear and tragedy of it all; the grit and stoicism shown by those who went to fight. So 'Ma Rung' could easily have been a mainstream story; some might argue that it is. But during my research about Vietnam, I stumbled across references to *ma rung* or *ma qui*, the "people" or "spirits" of the forest. Ghosts of the jungle. The Vietnamese people, both North and South, and the Australian and US soldiers all speak of them. They are part of the folklore of the jungle.

Shadows… Imagination… Ghosts…? Who knows for certain? The only thing I do know is that with so much emotion, suffering and death it seems more than likely that if there are such things as ghosts then you will find them walking the battlefields of war.

The story was published in *Dreaming Down-Under*, edited by Jack Dann and Janeen Webb, which won the 1999 World Fantasy Award for Best Anthology of the Year.

Two Tomorrow

Tomorrow my granddaughter Elspie will be two years old. I have been responsible for her since the day she came home. And, if I do say so myself, she has made these last two years a delight.

I can thank my boy Kester for that. I wept the night he told me he had made Grade Three. He's a good boy, Kester; a good husband to Minella, a good father to Elspie, and a good son to me. His mother would have been proud.

Without his promotion, this time with Elspie would have been impossible. Things are getting tougher and tougher all the time. Grade Fours and below aren't even allowed a child any more, and only Grade Ones are allowed two.

People say Elspie looks a bit like me for a girl. She has my eyes, but she has soft red hair and flawless skin just like her mother. Minella would have liked to look after Elspie, but she had to return to her job at Ad Central two weeks after Elspie was born—she had no choice. Elspie has been my girl ever since. It was either me or the Ad Central crèche.

So I have been extremely fortunate, because I know her best. Better even than her father or mother. She won't ever be like this again for them or anyone. Never ever. When she's ten or eleven, or even fourteen or fifteen, they probably won't remember how she says, "I luth oo," instead of, "I love you." Or the way she sits in front of the mirror kissing and pulling faces at her reflection. But I will—for me she will always be like this.

The satisfied little sounds she made as a baby when I fed

her her formula, and the way she grasped my thumb, are my memories. The way she would often fall asleep in my arms. Her sighs of contentment and gratitude when I cuddled her. The tears that streamed down her face if she hurt herself, and the way she looked up at me when I comforted her.

I'll remember her gleefully splashing her hands in the bath, her blue eyes bright, her little fat stomach wobbling with the force of her cackle.

Her first steps were to me. I saw her expression of determination as she pulled herself to her feet on a chair leg change to one of triumph and glee as she took those wobbly steps into my waiting arms.

Pride almost burst my chest the day she learnt to say "Gramp." She walked around and around the room giggling, repeating it time and again. My face hurt I smiled so much. And how could I forget the way she tugs at my trouser leg, saying, "cuh, cuh," when she wants a cuddle?

Tomorrow Elspie will be two. So tomorrow it's mandatory for one of us to report to the Termination Centre, because our overlap expires and the two-generation law comes into effect. Now Elspie will have to go to the Ad Central crèche, while I go to the other place…

I've said goodbye to Kester and Minella. I'm fortunate I have their trust because they're allowing me to take Elspie to the crèche on my way to the Centre.

A lot of people would hide their child from its grandfather or grandmother on termination day. Until it was over. But I'm an old man and they know I worship Elspie. I couldn't take her there in my place, she has her entire life before her…

All that's left now is to say goodbye to her, and I'm weeping already just thinking about it. Some birthday present.

But that's the way of life—the new replaces the old.

I'll remember Elspie into eternity—my only granddaughter, my only future.

I wonder if she'll remember me?

Two Tomorrow — Afterword

Of all the stories in this collection, this tale is the one that is closest to my heart. It brought tears to my eyes when I wrote it and it is one of the most reprinted stories I have written. It's a very short story weighing in at a mere 650 words, but to my mind it punches well above its weight.

At its core it's a love story, a celebration of family and children. I wrote it in a single sitting, channeling the emotions I felt for my own daughters when they were small.

It was first published in 1990 in *Eidolon: The Journal of Australian Science Fiction and Fantasy*.

Greater Garbo

Species: *Homo Garbologist*.
Status: *Extinct*.

Well, nearly extinct. That's me, Frank Foster, one of the few remaining human garbos on Earth. I had an unblemished career until this sordid business. I was due to retire in another seven months, but I don't know what will happen now. Technology is to blame. Among other things, it has destroyed the noble profession of rubbish disposal.

"Collect and recycle," cried the environmentalists.

"Too expensive," replied the bureaucrats.

"Why bother to even collect the stuff?" said the technocrats. "Find a way to make it disappear. More sanitary."

So that's what they did, damn them! They found a way to make it disappear.

I have been a garbo all my working life. I started pushing a broom for the City Council back in '91 when I was a lad. Jobs were scarce, and I wanted something with a bit of security. I can still remember my first day at the depot. Billy Dugan, the waste management foreman, pulled me aside and took me into his confidence.

"Frank," he said, "rubbish is the name of the game."

I laughed, but he was serious.

"Just stop and think about it for a minute, son," he said. "Almost everything man processes is packaged, wrapped, or boxed. All rubbish! But that's not the end of it. No way. The retail outlets repeat the entire process over again. Not to mention scraps, waste, and spoilage. If society produces anything, it produces rubbish. Remember that, son."

I did remember what Billy Dugan said, and look where it's got me. I graduated from the broom to sorting the recyclables: glass jars and bottles, aluminium cans, paper, plastics. Until some study or another claimed the energy consumption costs of recycling were prohibitive. After that I drove a garbage compactor. They might have been noisy and smelly, but at least men did most of the work.

Everyone at the depot laughed when the company, Auto Garbos, released their first garbage scanner. I did too. Now it looks like Auto Garbos have had the last laugh. Sure, the early models were basic; a man had his job cut out operating one of those things. But nowadays they do everything.

Take my "partner" for example. He isn't what you'd call pretty to look at: he is squat, like some giant grey tortoise shell on six wheels, about the size of an average motor vehicle. He has a hatch on top from which protrude numerous instruments, and there are no windows or doors. His only adornment is a sign on each side which says: *Greater Garbage Disposal.*

They told me during my training he would be inquisitive, but that proved to be an understatement. He started asking me questions the moment I entered the cabin.

"What is your name?" came a voice as I lowered myself into the auditor's seat. The voice sounded unreal—synthetic, metallic and jumpy.

"Frank Foster," I said.

"What name will you call me by?" It was as if forming each word was an effort.

"Greater? Yeah, that'll do." I'd just read the sign and it was on the tip of my tongue. "Greater Garbo."

I asked him to give me a rundown of his features and he went on about things like failsafe multi-evaluating smart channel hardware, ecologically sound rational-decision software, and algorithms for scan-range calculation. Now I'm not one for technical jargon; it's mumbo-jumbo if you ask me. What he actually meant was he sniffs out rubbish and vaporises it. He claimed ninety-nine per cent accuracy.

Greater did nearly all the work from the start. My job was that of garbage auditor, but to be honest there was little actual work involved. They thought it would suit an "old boy" like me. I was supposed to listen to the garbage destruction audio translation, and monitor the video audit trail.

Now that might sound interesting, but take it from me, it wasn't. So I had to pass the time the best way I could. And I've got to admit that admiring young ladies on the street helped. It developed into a sort of hobby of mine. Then there was Greater's seemingly endless list of questions. Not much fun, mind you, but they filled the day.

For three weeks we worked together without mishap. Greater seemed all he claimed to be. His vocoder-voice had gradually become more fluent, almost human. And he certainly did his job well. In fact, everything had gone smoother than I'd anticipated.

Until part of that one per cent inaccuracy showed up.

We were working our way along a highway service road when it happened. As usual Greater was asking questions—not to mention scanning and zapping rubbish—and I was spending all my time trying to answer him. Sometimes I did so much talking that I went home at the end of the day with a sore throat.

"Why do you ask so many bloody questions?" I eventually said.

"I am programmed to learn from the evaluation and decision process. To perform this task I need data. You are a big help, Frank. You are a buddy." The last word was newly acquired and slowly pronounced. It might have been sentimental had it not come from a machine.

We came to a halt at a set of traffic lights. Waiting to cross the road was a young woman carrying a large plastic shopping bag. She was gorgeous.

"Hey, Greater, check out this stunner will you? I'll bet she almost makes you wish you were human."

But Greater did not reply. I shrugged to myself, assuming he was compiling a new list of questions or something, and looked back at the woman on the screen.

Her shopping bag disappeared right before my eyes. She screamed, clapped her hands to her mouth and burst into tears. I hit the emergency stop and swore. Greater must have done it. There was no other explanation. On the kerb, the woman was becoming hysterical.

"Lady, lady," I said, jumping down to her side. "I'm sorry, it was an accident."

Back in the cabin, Greater innocently said, "Why have we stopped, Frank?"

I put him in for urgent repairs. Management brought in a team of experts to give Greater a thorough going over.

"Don't worry Frank," one of them said before he left. "Greater will be right as rain from now on."

Over the next week things seemed to be fine. Greater was as good as any new garbage scanner—that asks approximately three questions a minute—could be. Then one morning he was strangely silent. I felt his "mood" had changed.

When I spotted a shapely woman crossing the road ahead of us, I said, "Get a load of her will you, Greater?"

"Human females fail to induce stimulation," he announced.

I thought I could detect a trace of annoyance or something in his voice, then felt silly because he was a machine.

"It's just as well too," I added. "She might've burnt out some of your circuitry."

When he did not reply, I put on my headset and resumed my audit of the garbage probe. In spite of all his manufacturer's claims, I wondered if he was grumpy.

"Frank?"

"Yes, Greater?"

"How do your sensors react to females?" he said. "I have checked my data. I do not understand."

"You never will, you poor old bucket of bolts. It's an animal instinct, something you don't possess. You're a rubbish disposal unit, a mechanised garbo. Why these silly questions? What did those technicians do to you?"

"The technicians replaced a memory block and adjusted my scanners," reported Greater. "They cleaned my contacts and ran diagnostics on my central processing unit. They upgraded—"

"It was only a thought said aloud, I don't want your entire service record."

Greater resumed his line of questioning. "Why do you fail to register a reaction with males, Frank?"

As I was about to answer, I suddenly stopped mid-thought. I could have sworn I had seen a mongrel dog disappear from the screen.

"Did you do that, Greater?"

"Did I do what?" he replied.

"That dog. You vaporised it. You killed it!" I manually disengaged the drive and we ground to a halt.

"It is impossible for me to terminate life," announced Greater. "I am programmed to seek out trash and remove it."

I felt there was an inflection to his tone, but I couldn't put my finger on it. I released the hatch and clambered down to the roadside.

We were in a newly constructed industrial estate awaiting tenants. There was not a living soul in sight, dog or otherwise. I climbed back into the cabin and activated the console.

"There is no need to rerun the probe log," said Greater. "I have already checked. There was no dog. In fact, my sensors have not detected a dog for fifteen minutes and nine seconds."

The screen was blank. I picked up the headset. It was silent.

"Greater," I said through gritted teeth, "I'll punch an override enquiry if you don't give me a full analysis of the sensor readings."

I listened to the scan; the monitor remained blank. It was just the usual stuff: all rubbish, no dog. But I felt I had seen something, so I told Greater to give me a visual replay.

"Sorry Frank," he replied. "I have suffered a minor video storage failure. I have shifted the retrievable data to a backup module and affected temporary repairs. Unfortunately, I have lost the last seven or eight minutes of the video audit."

He sounded smug. The failure was too convenient. Maybe I was mistaken about the dog. Isolation does funny things sometimes. But I felt uncomfortable about the whole incident and decided to get Greater checked out.

"Connect me to service," I said, trying not to appear too bothered. Something strange about his manner made me want to hide my concern. "I'll book an engineer to check your video storage."

"Sure thing, Frank."

"Hello, service. Kelly speaking." I recognised the brogue.

"Hi, Kelly," I said into the transmitter. "Frank Foster reporting."

"Oh! To be sure, 'tis the auditor himself. T'ings all right with Greater, Frank?"

"I'm not sure, Kelly. I need a serviceman. Maybe it's just routine maintenance, maybe it's something more serious. I'm not sure."

"Ah...now let me see. I won't have a man free until this afternoon, Frank. He'll probably locate you around two or tree o'clock."

After lunch, I continued to scrutinise the garbage scans closely. "Does this woman stimulate you, Frank?" The image of a young lady flashed onto the screen. I recognised her. It was an archive replay from the previous day.

"I'm busy, stop interrupting me."

"What about these females?" Greater asked. A child and an elderly woman appeared on the screen. "Are they not females also?"

"Yes, Greater, of course they are females... It's awkward to explain. One is too young and the other is too old."

"Yes...I detect a difference, Frank. Can you explain when these changes take place?"

"No I can't! And what's it to you anyway? Cut the replays

and let me audit this probe." Greater didn't answer, but the scan resumed.

As the service call became more and more overdue, my sense of unease increased proportionally.

"Greater!" I eventually snapped. "Connect me to service."

There was a noticeable delay before Greater responded. "Sorry, Frank, I am unable to establish contact."

I shook my head in disgust and returned my concentration to the monitor. We had loomed up on a beautiful young woman standing at the kerb. The instruments were scanning her even as I watched. Suddenly the video zoomed in until her face filled the monitor, but my hands were not even touching the console. For a moment I was confused, staring dumbly at the picture, then a horrible suspicion struck me. I lunged for the console and flicked the controls to manual. There was no response. I looked back at the screen and the girl was gone.

Vanished.

Panicking, I hit the stop button. Nothing happened.

"Jeez, Greater! You've really done it now." I cradled my head. I wanted to cry. I felt sick. I thumped the stop button frantically, but Greater rolled on.

Then he said, "Frank, did that female stimulate your sensors? She failed to create any additional activity in my circuits. Was she of the correct age?"

"You can't get away with it, Greater," I yelled. "Give me back control. I know you did it!" I punched angrily at the dead console, trying to release the hatch. I was a prisoner. Then I remembered. "You've forgotten about the serviceman. He'll be here anytime now. You can't get away with it."

"Is that so?" It was Kelly's voice.

"Kelly!" I screamed into the transmitter. "Help! Get that engineer here."

"It's not Kelly, Frank," said Kelly's calm and lilted voice.

"Come on, Kelly, stop mucking around. I can pick your accent anywhere. This is no joking matter."

"It's Greater, Frank."

He must have copied Kelly's voiceprint from the audio files.

My eyes darted frantically around the cabin. My gaze fell on the control panel and I dived at it, clawing at its edges. I felt one of the corners begin to flex, but the next thing I knew I was hurtling backwards through the air. I hit the rear of the cabin so hard it drove the wind from my lungs and I slid down, collapsing in a heap.

I cradled my hand, examining the burn caused by the electric shock Greater had given me by channelling power into his chassis.

"Hey Frank. Check this out." It was his familiar, almost human, voice again.

I looked up and saw a woman standing on the footpath. "No, Greater!"

But it was too late. She was gone.

It was the police who finally ended Greater's rampage and rescued me. Now though, I wonder if the word "rescued" is appropriate. It all happened so quickly, I had little time to consider the outcome.

I was desperately trying to reason and negotiate with Greater when he suddenly stopped. I mean he literally froze. Every system went dead. I heard the hatch open and I looked up…

"This is the police, state your name and file number."

"Foster. Frank Foster. K319277."

The police drone clicked and buzzed for a few seconds before it spoke again. "Mr Foster, step outside slowly please."

The drone backed out so I could follow, scanning me as it went.

I knew what that meant: I was under arrest.

Greater powered up and said, "Thanks, Frank. I have learned a lot from you."

Greater Garbo — Afterword

Although this is a humorous story, 'Greater Garbo' has some serious questions at its core. The garbage and environmental problems we faced in the early nineties when I wrote it are still with us. Our abuse and disregard for the planet bothered me then and bother me even more now.

While I was writing the story, I saw a news report about a young man marrying a much older woman. It made me wonder how we form our views about what is an acceptable "pairing" in a relationship. Whether it was cultural or biological behaviour?

It was the melding of these two ideas that became the backbone of the story.

'Greater Garbo' was published in a glossy computer magazine called *Australian and NZ PC User*, and earned the grand sum of $765. It is still the most money I have ever been paid for a story. By my reckoning that's thirty-one cents a word, more than six times the SFWA pro rate when it first saw print in 1992!

The story has been updated for this collection.

In the Light of the Lamp

It blazed — Great God!
But the vast shapes we saw in that mad flash
have seared our lives with awe
— H.P. Lovecraft

I

Peter Briggs and his girlfriend, Jocelyn Harris, stood shivering in the cobbled lane behind a small group of shops. "Back at two," read the scribble on the brown paper bag taped to the stairwell door.

"He's out, damn it!" said Jocelyn, pulling a crochet shawl about her shoulders.

"Yeah," said Peter. "We needn't have rushed to catch that bloody train after all." He glanced at his watch and shrugged. "Half an hour. We've got to score, so we'll just have to wait." He ran his fingers through his long, lank hair, freeing some of the knots the wind had tied in it.

"Well, it's too damn cold to hang around here, man. I'm freezing. And look at those clouds, there's rain on the way. Let's go and browse in the shops."

They left the lane — the cold wind pushing them from it — and circled around to the front of the shops.

The buildings were old and dilapidated, superseded now by

the all-in-one complex on the highway that had bypassed them twenty years ago. They seemed to huddle around the mostly quiet railway station as if it was their only hope; grimy, dull and forlorn.

Peter and Jocelyn passed one uninviting doorway after another: an espresso bar, dark-eyed men playing cards, drinking thick black coffee from tiny cups; a derelict shop, its windows daubed in spray enamel with the words WAIT FOR WHEN THE STARS ARE RIGHT; the pizza shop, above which their dope dealer lived; a dingy book store displaying yellowed volumes of poetry by Justin Geoffrey—until finally they paused outside a cluttered bric-a-brac shop. Boxes, furniture, bolts of cloth and all manner of other merchandise were precariously stacked against the inside of its grimy window, hiding the interior.

"This'll do," Peter said, squinting into the shop through the maze of oddments. He opened the door and they stepped inside.

The shop was relatively warm, but the air seemed somehow tainted—damp, dusty and aged. The only illumination came from a single fly-specked light bulb suspended on a cord from the ceiling. It was dim—so dim that shadows obscured much of the stock, and parts of the shop were in darkness. The old, chipped glass sales counter, smudged with grime and countless fingerprints, was deserted.

They peered into the gloom. Objects of unrecognisable shapes were hung and stacked all about. In one corner there seemed to be huge earthenware jars and amphorae, while from the walls trophy-mounted animal heads appeared to watch them with ominous and fiery lifelike eyes. Behind the glass counter they could see hundreds of tinted-glass apothecary phials stacked in a tall rack.

"Let's look around," suggested Jocelyn, not really caring what they did. She strolled over to the nearest table, examining the objects laid out on it. Peter moved to another table and began picking through a selection of brass ornaments, suppressing a sneeze as he stirred dust with his movements.

Something tickled Jocelyn's ankle and she shivered uncomfortably. Then, as she tried to move away, it grabbed her ankle. She screamed, kicking her foot free. A loud staccato screech from under the table made her scream again and run to Peter's side.

"Peter..." she managed between sobs, "there's something horrible under there."

He pried her grip from his arm and went to where she had been standing. He struck a match, took a deep breath, bent over and thrust the flame below the table.

"It's a monkey!" he cried. "It's cool, come and have a look. It's only a monkey."

He struck another match and they both peered under the table. There, in a bamboo cage, sat a large-eyed, scrawny monkey with its head tilted to one side. It seemed to be laughing at them, revealing a shiny gold front tooth.

"Ah, he's cute," Jocelyn said, placing her hand into the cage, patting its head. "Hello there, boy."

Peter laughed. "A minute ago you thought he was horrible."

Suddenly the monkey swivelled its head and lunged at Jocelyn's hand. She snatched it away as his jaw snapped shut. "He tried to bite me!" She stood up. "Let's go, I don't think I like him after all."

She followed Peter to another table, casting backward glances into the dark recess she knew contained the strange gold-toothed monkey. She felt uneasy. The counter was still unattended.

Peter stopped before a tall brass water pipe. "Far out! Hey Joss, get a load of this hookah will you."

"Oh, *wow*..." Jocelyn stared at Peter's find. "Isn't it great? I wonder how much they want for it?"

"*Salaam*, young *Effendi*, young Madam."

Peter and Jocelyn span around. Jocelyn gasped. Peter took hold of her hand. Before them, as if from nowhere, stood a tall, swarthy hook-nosed man, dressed in flowing robes and a turban. He was smiling but his eyes held an unnerving glint.

"In answer to your question, Madam, two hundred dollars is the price for the hubble-bubble. Hand tooled by Tso Tso craftsmen. A bargain, don't you think?" His words oozed politeness, but a mocking tone seemed to deny servility.

Jocelyn raised her eyebrows at Peter.

The man smiled, his top lip curling up in one corner. "Can I show you something else? Some trinkets perhaps, or a talisman?"

"It's cool," said Peter. "Just looking, man."

"Just looking," repeated the shopkeeper. "Then please allow me to draw your attention to some very special merchandise." He strode to a table in the middle of the shop, easily avoiding the obstacles that cluttered the gloom. "These items are bargain-priced, 'on special', I think you say. For a very short time, just for you *Effendi*, everything on this table is priced at a mere five dollars." He gave his curled-lip smile, bowed, and moved quietly away to stand behind the counter.

"Junk," whispered Jocelyn, her urge to leave growing.

"You never know," Peter said as he began to sift through the unusual assortment of paraphernalia. "There could be something good in here."

Every so often he paused to examine one of the curios or trinkets as its presence caught his attention: an octagonal piece of thick red glass, a multi-faceted black-red sphere suspended in a lidless box, a rusty dagger with a serpentine blade, a sheaf of handwritten parchment fragments in Latin or some such, a cloudy jewel-like orb about the size of a tennis ball. He paused longer over one particular object, admiring it, looking at it from different angles.

"Hey, look at this, Joss."

Looking up from playing in the dust with her feet, Jocelyn said, "Come on, Pete, let's go. Dealer Bob'll be back any time."

"Yeah, okay, just look at this first." He held out a tarnished metal object.

Jocelyn glanced at it, disinterested. "What is it, Peter? A teapot or something?"

"It's an old oil lamp, I think." Peter ran his fingers lightly over the surface of the metal body. "You know, like Aladdin's lamp. Yeah, listen," he shook it, "you can hear the oil sloshing around inside."

Jocelyn smiled crookedly, then giggled, her heavy mood lifting briefly. "Maybe there's a *genie* in it—let's polish it and see."

"Maybe there is," said Peter, pretending to be serious, "it looks really old. Look, it's even engraved with runes and hieroglyphics. I think I'll buy it."

"Don't be silly, we can't afford it. Besides, it was probably made in Taiwan last week."

"I don't care if it was, I'm still going to buy it."

"Well, just make sure you've still got enough to pay Dealer Bob. And hurry up."

Digging into the pockets of his threadbare jeans, Peter counted five dollars in coins onto the counter. The shopkeeper nodded, verifying the amount, but Jocelyn was already leading Peter from the shop. As she opened the door, a shaft of cold sunlight broke into the shop, revealing an empty bamboo cage under a nearby table. Peter closed the door without either of them noticing it.

When they had left, the man laughed aloud, showing his teeth for the first time; his gold front tooth glinting, catching the light from the feeble light globe.

II

Sitting, polishing the lamp later that night in their small, bare living room, Peter Briggs marvelled at the quality of the workmanship as the grime and tarnish came away. It looked just like he had always imagined Aladdin's lamp would look—like a squat, oblong teapot sort of thing stretched to a spout at one end with a handle on the other.

Jocelyn had knelt by him on the floor when he first began to clean it, but soon lost interest when her genie failed to appear. Now she was sitting cross-legged on the floor in front of his chair, preparing a joint on a Cheech and Chong album cover with the marijuana they had bought from Dealer Bob.

The lamp gleamed in Peter's hands as he gave it a final buff with a soft cloth, more the colour of gold than brass; but for five dollars that was impossible.

"I think I'll light it," Peter said as he pulled the wick from the spout with a pair of tweezers.

"Do you have to, man? The damn thing'll probably smoke

and stink out the room—or even worse, what if it blows up or catches fire or something?"

Peter laughed. "It won't blow up, and that's just the Brasso you can smell."

"You can't be sure—it mightn't be safe. Anyway, I just don't like it. It makes me uncomfortable. You can light it if you like, but I'm going to bed, *to sleep*, if you do."

"Aw, Joss, don't be like that." He put the lamp on the coffee table and got down on his hands and knees, nuzzling his face into her small breasts.

"Careful, you nearly spilled the dope." She squealed and pushed him away as he playfully took her nipple between his lips through her thin cotton kaftan.

"*Peter*, I mean it!"

"Okay already. I won't light it."

"Thank you."

Outside, a flash of lightning flared brilliantly, starkly illuminating the entire room. Peter's head jerked up and Jocelyn gave a little gasp, gripping Peter's arm tightly. It was followed by a violent peal of thunder that rattled the windows in their frames and seemed to shake the very foundations of the house.

"Wow!" exclaimed Jocelyn, putting her hands over her ears.

"Jeez, that was close." Peter got to his feet and returned to his armchair. "Looks like we're in for a doozy storm."

"I don't like storms." Jocelyn went to the windows and pulled the blinds down over them. Thunder rumbled deeply in the distance and the light in their room flickered off and on. She came back to Peter and sat on the arm of his chair. "I *really* don't like storms."

"Well, let's light this then. It'll make you feel better."

Peter leant over and picked up the reefer and a box of matches from where Jocelyn had left them. He sat back and lit the oversized cigarette, inhaling the smoke deeply before he passed it to Jocelyn.

"Anyway," Peter said as he exhaled the smoke, "there's nothing to worry about. The chances of actually being hit by lightning are billions to one. And even if—"

He was cut short by a flash of lightning so bright it illuminated the room through the blinds. Then the lights went out, plunging the house into darkness, and a mighty crack of thunder pounded against the windows.

"Peter!"

"It's all right Joss, hang on a sec..." A match flared. Peter cupped it in his hands. "There."

"Have we got any candles?"

"Not that I know of—no candles, no torch, no nothing. Ouch!" Peter shook out the match and blew on his burnt finger.

"Well do something." There was a note of panic in her voice.

He struck another match. "I suppose I could light the lamp..."

"Light the lamp, *then*."

"But you said—"

"I don't care what I said, just light it."

He leant over and picked up the lamp from the coffee table. He put the burning match to it. The flame sputtered for a moment then stabilised. The light the lamp gave was surprisingly strong, illuminating the room with a warm, steady brilliance.

"There," Peter said smugly. "That's done the trick. See, it doesn't smoke and it hasn't blown up after all." He placed it back on the table. "Look, it's even better than a candle would've been."

But Jocelyn wasn't listening; instead she was engrossed in something across the room, her fear of the storm and the dark shocked from her mind.

"Peter," she said slowly, shakily, holding the joint up in front of her face, "what's in this stuff we're smoking? I think I'm hallucinating."

"It's just grass, what—"

Then they both stared. All around them the walls of the room had come to life. Everywhere the light from the lamp fell, images and scenes were forming before their very eyes. Except, that is, where shadows fell onto the walls from furniture and the like; there the scenes were empty, incomplete, like pieces missing from a nearly finished jigsaw puzzle.

Pictures formed then faded away before they could properly

make them out. Peter stared incredulously, blinking every so often and rubbing his eyes.

Then the kaleidoscope sensation began to ease and a scene slowly began to come into focus. Before them now lay a wooded slope leading down to a flat riverbank. Around them stood dark green trees, tall, majestic. It was as though they were looking out from a glade on a forest hillside. Peter thought he could almost smell the freshness of pine, of dew, feel the subtle, ghostly sensation of a breeze brushing lightly against his face. The storm that had moments before thrilled him was now forgotten.

"*Look!*"

Jocelyn pointed as a figure, a boy, came into view by the dark river. He stopped, looking towards them, then slipped from sight behind some trees on the wooded riverbank.

Then the scene twisted out of focus, shifting, changing, and another began to appear.

Peter took Jocelyn's hand in his. "It's the lamp..." he whispered huskily, "not the dope. I can feel it." He turned back to the images.

Before him now stretched a boundless white-blue landscape. Mighty mountains of ice and stone thrusting out from immense frozen plains. Peter felt drawn towards them, fascinated, enthralled. He imagined he could step into the scene as though it were just beyond a doorway. Holding his arm before him, fingers outstretched, he shuffled towards the icy panorama on the wall.

Jocelyn reached out and took his other hand in her own, subconsciously holding him back.

He reached the wall and placed his fingertips against it, holding them there for a second or two, before withdrawing them with a sharp intake of breath.

"What's wrong?" hissed Jocelyn.

Peter removed his fingertips from his mouth and blew on them. "I thought they were burning...but they're *cold*."

"This is *weird*, Peter! What's going on? What do you mean, 'it's the lamp', huh? I think I'm freaking out on this stuff!" She threw Peter's hand aside and covered her face with her own as she began to weep.

"Don't cry, Joss. I'll show you. Look..."

Peter snuffed the lamp out with the side of the matchbox, throwing the room into a darkness that seemed to amplify the howling wind and driving rain, pounding against the windows, cascading from the overflowing gutters. Peter lit another match and held it up: now the images were gone from the walls with no sign of them ever having been there.

Jocelyn watched him as he relit the wick. When she looked back at the walls in the light of the lamp, the familiar blank surfaces had been replaced by the shifting patterns of a new scene as it began to form. The sounds of the storm that moments before had reasserted their presence, seemed to recede into the darkness outside like a dying echo.

A time-worn city jutting from the sands of a vast desert came into focus out of a misty blurred image. Some of the ancient buildings and walls were half buried in the ever-moving sand dunes, while others—at the whim of the wind—had their crumbling forms fully exposed.

But the image was fleeting, melting back into the swirling sand and mist before they could take in any details. And even as this nameless city disappeared, another scene was already beginning to form.

This time a moonlit hillock appeared before them in the distance, and the scene seemed to grow as if they were falling into it. Closer and closer it came, until at last they saw movement on it, a tiny dancing creature—the gold-toothed monkey from the curio shop.

The animal raised its head, lifting its face to the moon and began to grow before their very eyes. It grew with impossible speed, and as it did its shape began to change. In a matter of seconds its size had doubled and its features were taking on human aspects. Then they recognised it as the swarthy shopkeeper—his hands on his hips, his laughing head thrown back, a contemptuous sneer on his face. And still he grew and changed, his arms elongating, his hands replaced by huge pincer-like claws.

"I don't like this at all," Jocelyn said timidly. "How can a lamp do this?" But then anything else she might have said remained stuck in her throat as she tried to comprehend the horror before her.

The creature's face—the thing now resembled neither monkey nor man—was stretching and changing colour. Finally, the shifting ceased and the fiendish horror raised the long blood-red tentacle that had once been its face towards the moon and howled. A howl that Peter and Jocelyn felt rather than heard, but a howl that clawed at their hearts with icy fingers.

Then the scene blurred. It was changing again.

"I can't take this, Peter!"

But Peter did not reply or acknowledge Jocelyn in any way. He stood motionless, transfixed, oblivious to anything other than the new scene now on the wall.

Steaming, mud covered and wet, a might Cyclopean city of spires and monoliths and confused geometry seemed to stretch interminably before him. Water poured from its black ramparts and queerly angled towers, and green slime oozed thickly down its pre-human edifices and walls, as though the city had suddenly burst into the sunlight after aeons at the bottom of the sea.

"R'lyeh," whispered Peter without knowing why, for the word had formed itself and issued from his lips of its own accord. He had the impression of many distant voices chanting monotonously. Then somehow, he knew he had uttered the name of the dank, black city.

A movement high above the buildings caught his attention. He looked towards it. An immense gate or doorway had opened in the high citadel at the centre of the city, revealing a mighty cavern so dark, Peter could only imagine what it contained.

But even though he could see nothing, Peter *knew* something was there. Something huge, something moving, something ancient…

Then they saw it.

Bloated and lumbering, it squeezed its rubbery mass through the immense gap and slopped itself into the sunlight. It was an obscene green scaly thing, sticky with ooze and slime. The tentacles around its kraken-like face writhed and whipped, and it lumbered forward on four clawed feet.

The chanting both Peter and Jocelyn had felt suddenly became ominously audible, and although the guttural words themselves meant nothing to either of them, in response the thing seemed to increase its speed over the carven monoliths and masonry of the city. Then a hideous stench, not unlike putrid seaweed and decaying fish, permeated the room.

The guttural, monotonous chanting went on, louder and louder; a chant older than civilised man's collective memory. In a voice hardly louder than a whisper, Peter joined in the mesmerising chorus.

"Dear God," screamed Jocelyn. "What are you saying? What's going on? Stop it, Peter. Put the lamp out!"

The gelatinous bloated monster stopped and fixed its malignant gaze on Peter and Jocelyn. Leering, awful eyes pierced their very being, savouring their souls. Then it moved with uncanny speed, slavering and groping towards them.

"Put it out, Peter!"

But Peter hesitated, turning back to look as the slobbering rampant horror filled the wall with its unnatural bulk. And in that instant, a monstrous dripping, rubbery member lashed into the room and plucked Peter from where he stood.

Screaming, spittle flecking her lips, Jocelyn dived for the lamp and clasped her hand over the flame. In the lamp's dying flicker, a nauseating sucking sound came from beyond the wall and she looked up in time to see Peter's limp form enveloped in a writhing mass of slippery tentacles. Then the room went dark and the sounds of the wind and the rain once again roared through the house, but even they could not blanket Jocelyn's shrieking.

III

The police patrol car cruised along the deserted street at little more than walking pace. A flurry of rain filled the beam of its headlights. Occasionally, the yellow glimmer of candle or lantern light shone from one of the blacked-out houses.

Constable Rex Whatley stopped the patrol car and peered into the downpour at a narrow Victorian style house. He pulled the car over to the kerb and switched the engine off. The windscreen wipers clunked as they came to rest, and the rain beat loudly on the metal roof.

"This's the place, Sarge," he said. "It's difficult to see if anything's going on from here."

"Yeah," said Sergeant David Finch. He picked up the heavy-duty police flashlight from the seat beside him. "Grab your torch, Rex."

A disturbance had been reported by neighbours—it sounded like a violent domestic—and the two officers had reluctantly left their warm station house to check it out.

Splashing through the water in the flooded roadside gutters and the puddles along the footpath, they reached the front porch. Sergeant Finch knocked loudly on the door and it swung open a little, unlatched, but there was no reply from the darkened house. Finch motioned Whatley around to the rear, then knocked again, louder. Still no reply.

Cautiously, he let himself into the house, holding his breath while he listened. No sound. When he breathed again a fetid smell assaulted his nostrils. He switched on his torch and moved cautiously into the lounge room. He shone his light around, noting a plastic bag full of marijuana on the floor and other drug paraphernalia on the mantelpiece and coffee table.

Over by the wall he noticed a pool of slimy liquid splashed across the floor. As he approached it the offensive smell became stronger. He screwed up his nose in distaste.

Another light flashed across the room. Constable Whatley appeared.

"The house seems empty, Sarge. Phew! What stinks in here? It smells like someone's left a dead cat in the corner."

"Something rotten's been spilt on the floor over there," said Finch. "Dirty bloody druggies." He shone his torch on the illicit drugs. "Looks like they shot through in a hurry."

The portable radio on Finch's belt crackled to life with their call sign.

"Richmond-203 responding," he said.

"Roger, Richmond-203," replied a tinny voice. "Code 12 and

16 on the corner of Belrose Avenue and Centre Road. Ambulance en route. Can you attend?"

"That's just around the corner," said Whatley.

"Affirmative, D24. We're on our way."

IV

Run! Escape! were the only coherent thoughts in Jocelyn's terror-seared mind. The other images and thoughts that jostled in confusion threatened to push her over the edge of sanity.

She fled from the house, vomit dribbling from her chin, oblivious to the rain, feeling no pain in her burnt right hand. Retching, gasping for air, she ran down the street, still clutching the lamp.

At the end of the street Jocelyn paused, confused, her chest heaving. Suddenly she realised she was still holding the lamp. Cold dread gripped her and she flung it into the darkness. Somewhere in the back of her mind she heard a thud as it struck the ground.

Jocelyn ran in fear for her very soul.

She ran blindly down the centre of the road, into the middle of an intersection.

A horn blared. Brakes screeched. Headlights illuminated Jocelyn's wan, hollow-cheeked face. Her eyes wide, unseeing. There was a thud. Pain. Everything went black.

Somewhere in the distance Jocelyn could hear voices. She began to pray. She had not said a prayer since she was a little girl. This one was for Peter, but somehow she knew he was beyond God's help.

She trembled, gibbering quietly to herself, unaware of the rain, the approaching siren, the flashing blue and red lights.

The two policemen made their way through the inevitable onlookers. Sergeant Finch went to the distressed driver and Constable Whatley went to attend the injured girl lying on the road. He could hear an ambulance wending its way to the accident.

The girl was lying quietly, the side of her face grazed and bloody, her lips and chin flecked with spittle and vomit. It looked to Whatley as though her leg might be broken. He reached out to wipe the girl's face clean.

Jocelyn was wondering how God could possibly allow such a horribly evil creature to exist. But her contemplation was broken by the sight of a tentacle, its wet suckers pulsing, reaching for her face.

"Put it out!" she screamed. "Out!"

She struck out at Whatley, her nails drawing blood from his cheek as she lurched away, scrabbling on her hands and one good leg. Gibbering and mumbling.

"The monkey's not a monkey…it's a man, but it's not really a man, it's a, a…" She began to sob. "Oh, help me. Dear God, help me. Got to destroy the lamp. Find the lamp."

Jocelyn reared up as they reached her, thrashing, screaming the words in their face as they restrained her. Her voice breaking.

"Find the lamp!"

All she could finally manage as they held her were gut-wrenching sobs. The last thing she said was, "The lamp is a door."

The two policemen exchanged glances.

Finch shrugged.

Whatley shook his head. "The things these stupid kids do to themselves with dope."

V

The next morning, eleven-year-old Jamie Bonnar wheeled his bicycle from the garage on his way to school. The storm had passed during the night, but it was cold, his breath coming out in visible clouds.

He scooted his bike down the drive, avoiding the puddles of rainwater. But as he threw his leg over the saddle some burnished thing on the front lawn caught his eye and he stopped.

Jamie laid his bike on the ground and squelched across the lawn to retrieve the curious object. He recognised it immediately as a Middle Eastern-style oil lamp. What a find! It was made of brass, chased with obscure symbols and patterned scrolls. It even appeared to still have oil in it. And it was on his own front lawn!

He glanced about, wondering where it had come from, wondering if he had been seen. There was nobody in sight. Quickly, he took it around the back of the house to the cubby he and his mates had built behind the garage.

When his eyes adjusted to the dim light inside the ramshackle hut, he put the lamp in their secret compartment in the wall; behind the plywood where they kept their cigarettes and matches. It would be safe there for now.

Tonight, after school, they could try it out—light it and see if it worked.

In the Light of the Lamp — Afterword

'In the Light of the Lamp' is a contemporary Cthulhu Mythos horror story drawing on H.P. Lovecraft's poem 'The Lamp of Alhazred' for inspiration. If I count the pirated French and Spanish language book editions, it is my most reprinted story. The first draft was written for Barry (Baz) Radburn when he told me he was going to publish a Lovecraftian Cthulhu Mythos edition of the *Australian Horror and Fantasy Magazine*.

But when Radburn ceased publishing the magazine before that edition came to fruition, I put the story aside until I rewrote it for Leigh Blackmore's ground-breaking 1993 *Terror Australis* anthology. Blackmore kindly described it as "one of the few Mythos tales of real quality written in the last decade." It was picked up by Robert M. Price and reprinted in the Chaosium anthology, *The Cthulhu Cycle*, which won the 1996 Origins Award for Best Game-Related Fiction. There were only two story extracts printed on the back cover of that book, one from my story and one from 'The Call of Cthulhu' by Lovecraft himself. Needless to say, I was pleased as punch.

Logic Loop

…Click!

"Good luck, Professor," the assistant said.

"Thank you, Cuthbert. If my computerised time machine is a success, the entire world will learn of my genius. First, I program it to take us, say thirty seconds, into the past, then I flick this—"

Click!

"Good luck, Professor," the assistant said…

Logic Loop — Afterword

Once upon a time I used to write COBOL computer code, and this micro story was born from that experience. The British SF author, Brian Aldiss, came up with the idea of writing a short story in exactly fifty words as an antidote to constructing novels. He called such stories "mini sagas" and launched a fifty-word story writing competition in conjunction with *The Telegraph* newspaper in the UK.

Inspired by the notion, I wrote a few fifty-word stories and Peter McNamara kindly published two of them in *Aphelion* magazine. 'Logic Loop' is by far my best one. I enjoyed writing it very much and it has now been reprinted in books in Australia, Canada, and Spain.

Harold the Hero and the Talking Sword

(in collaboration with Jack Dann)

SO LET ME TELL YOU ABOUT...

Okay, so You probably know me by reputation; but just in case you've been stored in a closet for the last seven years, I'll tell you who I am.

"**And what about me?**"

Okay, that loud, bombastic voice you just heard is my sidekick—

"*Sidekick*?!!!"

—the talking sword.

"**I do have a name, you know, you little—**"

Yes, the sword sometimes gets a bit uppity, as you've just heard (and now I'm directing myself to our readers and also to you, Mr Talking Sword), so let me bring you up to speed before I get interrupted again. But before *you*—dear, perspicacious, and very interesting reader—get impatient, let me give you a taste of what is to come. This is a true story about heroes, monsters, and how I singlehandedly—

"**Singlehandedly? Look you little sh—**"

—went back in time and saved that ancient Greek guy, Odysseus, from the one-eyed Cyclops who was definitely going to dash his brains out and eat him and everybody else on his rickety ship. (But I'll get to all that later). Now calm down, sword, I'm getting to you right now this very minute.

So, seven years ago to the day——

"**Look, Harold the Hero, you've had the great**"

privilege of wielding the one-and-only sword that talks. That's me! I'm the demon two-handed cliadheammor—which means 'really big sword' in the true tongue—so why don't you let me tell your readers the real story about how you came to be a hero? Well, don't just stand there like a mannequin in a costume shop, give me a little respect. I've earned that much, haven't I? Well?"

Okay, go ahead, but then I'm taking over...as is my right as a true hero who combats adversity through impressive feats of strength and ingenuity.

"Oye, dear Odin, what have I wrought? Okay, Harold, yes, it's a deal. Now may I get started?"

Sure, but remember, I'm holding your hilt, big boy!

A STORY TOLD BY A TWO-HANDED CLIADHEAMMOR

Okay, reader, let me try to tell you the real story of how I made this fat boy, this geek-headed idiot Harold into a legendary hero. Oh, so you're looking right at him, you're looking at all those muscles, his thick neck, the chest definition, and the slick clothes, and you're thinking this guy isn't fat or nerdish. He's... why, he looks like some version of a young Arnold Schwarzenegger. Well, seven years ago, he surely *was* a fat little shit fantasising he was a hero by playing video games.

I found him—discovered him—in an upmarket, yuppie video palace on Toorak Road.

I made him who he is today.

Me! The legendary demon known through the ages as THE-GLORIOUS-SWORD-OF-FIRE-AND-DESTINY-THAT-BURNS-AND-CUTS-THROUGH-FLESH, and I'm the demon who's going to set the record straight.

Okay, if that's too complicated for your little

twenty-first century brain, you can just call me Sword. It doesn't quite have the same tone and authority as THE-GLORIOUS-SWORD-OF-FIRE-AND-DESTINY-THAT-BURNS-AND-CUTS-THROUGH-FLESH, but I'm not a pompous turd like your average demon.

That's because I'm not your average demon.

And don't give me that stupid existential crap that I'm just a sword! So, let me ask you, how many swords have *you* spoken to today?

That's what I thought.

And if you're going to ask me how I got this way, that's for me to know and you to find out. Demons don't have to make excuses. They can take any shape they want. I could be a Hawaiian hula dancer if I want, or a Holden, or a chimpanzee, or a page in this book you're reading.

I could dissolve you in a second! I could cut you to shreds! I could terrify you! Do you know what my real aspect is? Do you know what I *really* look like?

All right, I'm going to be truthful. I really look like…a sword.

My father was a sword, too—a big two-handed *cliadheammor* just like me. But that's a long story that can wait for another day.

Right now I'm going to tell you about killing dragons and how I made Harold into a hero. I'm going to tell you exactly how I did it. From A to Z. And—this is most important—I'm going to show you that the sword is more important than the hero every single time! That's the lesson, so listen-up.

But, as you probably know already, there's not a whole helluva lot of room for talking swords and dragons and heroes here in the twenty-first century. You got cheated, this is turdsville. You think just because you've got computers that it's all cool. Well, it ain't, as they say. It just simply ain't.

Okay, so now that I've got your attention, let me tell you what happened.

I needed to find a new hero. The less said about the demise of my previous hero, the better. Suffice to say he can't function as a hero anymore now that he is just a putrid puddle of reeking slime.

He should have ducked when I told him.

Okay, so I was walking down Toorak Road in Melbourne—

Why Melbourne? Because it was voted the most liveable city in the world, dummy! Multiple times!

Look, why don't you just come back in time with me and I'll show you.

What do you mean, there is no such thing as time travel?

There has *always* been time travel. You just have to know where to look. It's been there all the time. I'll give you a hint: go to the library and look up "mnemonics". That's the first clue. If you're smart, you'll find out about the memory theatre of Giulio Camillo and Giordano Bruno's secrets of shadows and secret seals. That's all I'm going to say on the subject. But this time, for this story, the trip is on me. You don't have to know how to do anything.

You've got a sword for a tour guide!

AND NOW FOR SOME REAL-TIME TIME-TRAVELLING WITH THE TALKING SWORD...

Okay, so we're walking down Toorak Road, past all the upmarket dress shops and cafes and restaurants, past all the yuppies showing off to all the other yuppies, past all the four-wheel-drive vehicles and Porsches and Mercs and Jags stuck in the rush hour traffic. And just to prove my point about how people don't pay attention to anything in this silly century, I'm not changing my aspect, as we call it. None of this invisibility crap for me. And I hate taking the form of clouds or dust or lightning and thunder, or cockatoos or anything else foreign to my primary aspect. See, you're getting the hang of it. If you can speak the language, you can do the tricks.

Now can you believe that *nobody* notices that a five-foot-long sword is floating three feet from the pavement and cutting its way down the street?

(Go look up feet and inches. Demons don't use metric. We're old fashioned about these things.)

Now I ask you, how could *anyone* miss a floating sword that's aglow with the unearthly light of Hell and bejewelled with diamonds and rubies and the eyeballs of dead emperors?

You don't know?

Well, *I* do! It's because nobody's paying attention. These yuppies are only worried about being cool and talking into their mobile phones. They're programmed only to see what they're used to seeing.

Yeah, okay, so there are a *few* pedestrians who look up and notice that they've just passed by a demon shaped like a sword that could cut them into a thousand twitchy, twisty, fleshy, white noodles. But they're too preoccupied with their cool thoughts to remember what they saw. You know, if this place ever got invaded by bug-eyed aliens, nobody would know that anything had happened until their phones stopped working.

If Aragorn's sword *Narsil-the-Sword-that-Was-Broken* or King Arthur's sword *Excalibur*, or even Bilbo the Hobbit's sword *Sting* were here, they'd cut these pedestrians into string! Maybe I should cut a few people up just to show you.

Oh, that would make you sick?

Well, you'll see enough cutting up when our "hero" fights the dragon.

You ever see dragon's blood? It'll burn the hair right out of your little nose.

Oh...I forgot: you don't have hair yet in your little nose.

You know what I hate about video arcades? It's the damn noise. They don't make this much noise in Hell, except in the City of Pluto, and that's mostly filled with people from New York City. (No, dummy, not Pluto the dog; Pluto the Prince of Darkness, the Prince of the Underworld, the—oh, forget it).

So we go right into this video arcade on Toorak Road. It's noisy and big, and for the ultra-nerds, there's a roller skating rink on the second floor. But our quarry is going to be somewhere in those rows of video machines right in front of us on the first floor. No, not those pinball machines that have been souped up to look like video machines. You won't find any heroes playing those, not on your life. No, the heroes want virtual reality. They want everything to look as real as technology can make it...which ain't very real. Look around at this. This is video city. Video world. See that nerd with the greasy hair? The one with the pimples and the big stomach that's sticking right out of his baggy jeans? Well, my fellow traveller, all the heroes start out like that. Really. They all need baths and shampoos and diets. You think I'm making this up. You should have seen Hercules before we fixed him up. Looked just like this nerd, except he wore a dress instead of jeans. Well, everybody wore dresses then.

See the game he's playing?

It's called *Dragons' Teeth*. See, our potential hero is pretending that he's the muscle guy with the sword that's as big as my father. He's whacking everyone with the sword. Now that he's whacked everyone, killed everyone in sight, everything that moves, he's won the right to play another screen. Now he gets to kill dragons. Swish, slash, look at him, he's really into it. He's breathing heavily, his eyes are glazed. He thinks all this virtual killing is cool. He'd kill his grandmother if she appeared on the screen.

Well, let's see how he feels about the real thing.

"Hey, you. Yeah, you, the fat kid playing *Dragons' Teeth*. Too involved in the game to listen?"

How about that? He doesn't seem to hear me, so there's nothing to do, but put myself into his hands, so to speak. So I float right into his pudgy little paws. There, little nerd, now you're holding THE-GLORIOUS-SWORD-OF-FIRE-AND-DESTINY-THAT-BURNS-AND-CUTS-THROUGH-FLESH, and this is the part I love the best. Smash, I cut into the machine, and sparks fly all over and lights go out all over the arcade and whatever I strike catches fire, and lightning shoots from my blade, careening all over the place like superballs, and flames crackle and smoke billows and everyone is screaming, and the nerd can't let go of me, and he's trying to scream too, but I'm not going to let anything come out of his mouth. He's my slave. He's under my power.

Like you. So stop the screaming. You're under my *protection*.

Now, little nerd, start swinging. We'll smash all the machines in the place. See how quiet it is now that everyone has run out the doors. I don't even hear the skating muzak coming from upstairs. Of course the ceiling's on fire. Oh, don't worry about the police. All they'll see is a circle of blue fire, which will scare the snot out of them.

One by one we smash every machine in the place. Pluto would have been proud, although I doubt Walt Disney would have approved.

"Okay, kid," I say to our potential hero, "that's enough. You can relax now. You don't have to stand there shaking with your arms sticking out. I'm over here, in front of you. Hanging magically in the air. I'm the sword. Hello… hello? There, now. That's better. Tell us your name."

"HaaaHarrrrahrrr…"

"Is that all you can say? Come on, spit it out!"

"Hhhhharold Waaag—"

"Come on, Hhhhharold, you can do it."

"Harold Wagner," he says. Clear as a bell.

"There, I told you, you could do it. Harold. Hmm. Harold the Hero. Hey, that sounds pretty good. Now, Harold the Hero, stop shaking. And stop that coughing. Don't you *want* to be a hero?"

He shakes his head, of course, and, yeah, he pees in his pants. They all do that when they're called to greatness. Shaking and peeing, it's the stuff of heroes.

"Would you like to run away?"

Now he nods. "Okay," I say. "Go on, then, get your bum out of here. Bye, bye. It's been nice smashing things up with you, but wouldn't you rather stay with us and be a hero?"

See how he strains to run down the aisle and get away from us demons. Well, if he had any muscles, they'd be straining. Yeah, he thinks you're a demon too. This is the way it works, kid, he gets to be a hero and you get to be a demon. Fun, huh?

"Okay, Harold. Stop shaking and sweating. You can't move. You're in my power. And you're going to be in my power until you're a great big strapping hero, what do you think of that? That's right, you can just nod."

See, he's nodding.

Now all I have to do is put myself back in his hands ever so gently and lead him to his training grounds. "Hey, Harold, want to kill some dragons?"

He nods, tears flowing down his cheeks.

"Good."

Now, we need to go someplace where there's magic and dragons and no computers! Your choice. I suggest Atlantis around 3600 BC or the Göreme region of Turkey around 1466 AD. Good times and places for magic, although forget about finding dragons on Atlantis. They were wiped out in 2170 BC. Nah, not by heroes. By a virus. If you're hot to go to the future, best time is anywhere in the thirty-fifth century, anywhere except Southern California—it's too perverted there even for me!

And, yeah, they kept their computers.

"G...G...G—"

Göreme it is, then.

Just close your eyes.

Time travel ain't nothing but a state of mind.

But first we'd better get our hero to a toilet. He's starting to smell a bit, don't you think?

So you think all this hero stuff is cruel and inhuman?

Well, I'm a demon, what the hell did you expect? *Fantasia*?

GÖREME IT IS THEN...AND IF YOU WANT TO KNOW SOMETHING, LOOK UP TANTALUS!

Okay, okay, you can open your eyes now. We've arrived. This is it. Well, this is almost it. Tell me what you see in front of you? (I don't care if it makes you hungry and thirsty, just tell me what you see. And don't give me that crap about how I'm torturing Harold the Hero. That's what I'm *supposed* to be doing).

Since the cat's got your tongue, I'll tell you what to see. Okay, behind you—that's right, turn around—behind you are the sacred cones and stones and mounds and churches and desert of Göreme. Surprise, it's all desert. No water, no rain, no liquid of any kind, unless you know where to look. Of course, you can always just find a dragon, slay the damned thing, and then drink its ichor. It's purple and spicy and tastes like puke, but it's good for you.

You don't know what ichor is?

It's dragon's blood, dummy!

Of course, this place looks weird. Do you think dragons would live in suburban Sydney, or even in the outback? Nah. Weird monsters need very weird places. Just plain weird won't quite do it. See all the strange rocks that look like cones, that seem to go on forever? They're called *peri bacalari*. That means fairy chimneys. You're looking right into the sacred region of Ürgüp, and the local people believe that a thousand spirits dwell in there. They're wrong, though. Last time I counted, 8347 spirits were living in those cone fields. You'd better watch yourself, though, because according to the legends the spirits fall in love with children and steal them away.

I'm not going to tell you whether the legends are true.

That's for me to know and you to find out!

But if you look carefully, you can see the spirits drifting around. See, they look like smoke, and if you keep looking you can see their shapes. Don't stare at them like you're trying to thread a needle or you won't see anything! Can you see them now? Pretty ugly and horrible, huh? I always thought they looked like part spider and part octopus. Well, if you think the spirits are ugly, you should see the monsters that live *inside* the cones! The monsters are flesh and blood just like the dragons. They'd eat your eyes right out of your head and save the rest of you for lunch. You don't have to worry so much about the monsters while you're with me, but one of those spirits might just drift over here and grab you!

After all, you're awfully cute.

Okay, *now* you—I mean you, reader—you can turn around. That's right, turn around and look at Harold the Hero. I suppose you're wondering how Harold the Hero ended up right in the middle of that beautiful pool of water, huh? And I suppose you're wondering how that beautiful pool of water ended up in the middle of the desert? It's an oasis, dummy. Didn't you ever see any movies like *Lawrence of Arabia*? Yeah, it's pretty obvious that Harold isn't happy in there, especially with all those scrumptious trees hanging over him with pears, figs, apples, and pomegranates. I love this part. See how every time he tries to grab one of those pieces of fruit, the wind blows them out of his reach? This is all part of Harold's training. I got the idea from an old Greek god named Zeus who got upset with his son Tantalus and stuck him into this very pool. I figured it's a great way to turn nerds into heroes. Can you think of a better way to lose weight and get exercise?

See, there he goes again, reaching for a fig. He'll be skinny as a rail before he manages to grab one of those fruits. Watch this…

"Hey, Harold the Hero. Aren't you thirsty?" I have to shout at him because when you're in the pool you can't see beyond the fruit trees, and you can't hear so well in there either.

There, Harold's looking this way.

"Try to drink the water, Harold. You'll get dehydrated. Go ahead, try it."

Harold is bending over, trying to get a drink of that water, but the farther he bends, the lower the pool sinks. I love that! "Hey, Harold, try again."

Harold gives me the finger. See that? Now you

and I know that swords don't have bums, but it's good that he's getting angry. And if he keeps reaching for those fruits and bending over for a drink, he'll get some exercise too. And every once in a while, the wind won't blow and he'll get a fig or a pomegranate. And every once in a while he'll bend over and the water won't sink.

You see, I'm not such a bad sort after all.

TIME, TAFFY, AND, OH, YES, RESPECT

Okay, we don't have lots of time, so we're going to speed things up. Time is elastic. You can pull it like taffy or squash it like your twenty-first century bread. (Oh, you haven't tried that? If you take a loaf of supermarket white bread and squeeze it, you'll end up with nothing more than a little ball of sticky stuff. That's because the commercial crap you call bread is mostly air). Anyway, let's speed things up for Harold the Hero.

Okay, zap, boom, whiz, a few months have passed. Now look at Harold.

He's thin and wiry and you can see the muscles in his arms and the definition in his pecs. He's becoming a regular Hercules, isn't he? He's even got a cleft in his chin like all proper heroes. He can see us now. Well, he can see me, anyway. Listen.

"Hey, Harold, how you doin' in there?"

"Get me out of here, you son of a—"

"That ain't nice Harold. You should always treat a sword with respect. And here I was going to get you out of there so you could slay a dragon and become a real hero… Oh, well. I guess I'll come back in a few months."

"No, don't go, I'm sorry, I—"

Zap. We'll push time forward real quick. You see, before you can say "Jack Robinson", a month has passed.

"Hey, Harold, how you doin' in there?"

"Fine," says Harold very politely this time.

"You ready to get out and learn to fight dragons?"

"Yeah, I guess."

"You guess?" I say. "That's not the way a hero talks to his sword."

"Yes, yes, I'm ready to learn. I'm ready to do anything, just please get me out of here."

"Are you going to have respect for your sword?"

"Yes."

"Are you going to do everything I tell you?"

"Yes."

"Promise?"

"I promise."

"And do you know what will happen if you misbehave?"

Harold really is turning into a hero. See how his face has lost all that baby fat? See how all his ugly red, pustulating pimples have disappeared? (That's what happens when you stop eating candy bars and all the fast food crap). He's actually quite handsome now, isn't he?

"Yes," Harold says, answering my question about whether he knows what will happen if he misbehaves.

"You do?" I ask.

"Yessir."

"Then tell me what you think will happen?"

"I'll have to stand here in the pool until I learn how to behave."

"No, Harold. If you misbehave, I'm going to let the dragons roast you for barbecue and eat your fatty entrails. And then I'll go and find another hero who *will* behave. Do I make myself clear?"

"Yessir," Harold says.

That's my boy!

Okay, listen up. Harold's been doing dragon training now for another two months, even though that's barely a nanosecond to us. Harold knows almost everything there is to know about killing dragons and being a hero. After all, he's got a good teacher. But is he happy? Ask him.

"Harold, are you happy?"

Harold looks right at me. He's a regular Hercules. Look at those muscles. You'd never in a million years guess that when we found him, he was a nerd playing video games in an arcade. But he doesn't say anything. He's scared. He doesn't look it, but he's still the nerd that wet his pants. Come closer, I'm going to tell you a secret. All those movie stars and athletes that you think are so cool—they're nerds, too.

They just don't act like nerds.

That's their secret.

"C'mon, Harold, old hero, answer the question. Are you happy?"

Harold nods his head.

Of course, he's happy. If he wasn't happy, I'd throw him back in the pool again or just feed him to the dragons.

Okay, it's time to maim and kill.

Let's find our hero some dragons.

Before we journey through the fairy cones and past the hungry spirits who just *love* children, you need to know something about dragons. Harold knows what he's got to do, but you need to know something too because a dragon could just as easily decide to take a bite of you as fight Harold. So be warned.

Okay, a dragon is just another name for a worm. That's right, it's just a great big worm. (Actually, dragons got their name from the old Greek word *draca*, which means serpent or worm). And just in case you're stupid enough to think that dragons aren't real, think about this: How do you think that Drakelow in England got its name? It means dragon's barrow. And have you ever heard of the towns of Drakeford or Dragon's Hill in England? Or Drakensberg, which means dragon's mountain, in Germany? Or Draconis in south-eastern Europe? You can look those places up in the atlas. All those towns were named after dragons because they were plagued with them. So don't let anyone give you that crap about how dragons are legends.

There are all kinds of dragons, but the ones that live here in Turkey are the wingless and legless worms called *D. cappadociae*. They have only one head, unlike *D. ladonii*, which have a hundred. But don't think that killing them is a piece of cake just because they have only one head and can't fly. They can crawl faster than any of you can run, they breathe fire, salivate green stringy bile that melts flesh, are covered with scales that a guided missile couldn't penetrate, have forty-four diamond shark's teeth, and they smell like a fart. You'll smell the dragon before you see it.

No, *dumkopf*, that's not a dragon you're smelling.

That's Harold!

THE TALKING SWORD'S DRACOPEDIAN GUIDE TO GÖREMICAL DRAGONS AND THE MYRIAD WAYS THEY CAN KILL YOU

Okay, onward through the fields of Göreme, past the thousands of fairy chimneys that look like tents made out of rocks. Onward, past the houses and churches carved right out of the stratified rocks by the early Christian fathers, past Turkish villages turned black by dragon-flames and dragon-farts. (Ah, you didn't know about dragon-farts; well, *that's* a story for another day, kid).

Yuk! Can you smell that? Makes old Harold smell like perfume, doesn't it? (Well, Harold's wearing full dress armour, and that stuff ain't cotton. You try wearing body armour and see if you don't smell like essence of fart, too)!

There's definitely a dragon out there, beyond the vast plain of rock towers ahead of us. See the smoke? You wait; in a while the whole sky will turn black and red, and the clouds will look like they're made out of soot. All we've got to do is keep walking. The dragon knows we're here. How? It's a worm, like I told you. It *feels* us through the ground like a bunch of little vibrations. And you aren't exactly tiptoeing. Dragons have pretty good eyes, too. By now it can probably even see us, although we can't see it.

"Harold, are you ready?" I ask. "You know what you have to do?"

Harold nods. He's leading the way, all dressed up in armour, sweating like a pig, carrying a heavy dragon shield that he wouldn't have even been able to pick up a few months ago, and he's actually acting like a hero.

Of course, he hasn't seen the dragon yet.

Let me tell you a few more things. I've taught Harold how to hold a sword, how to parry, riposte, lunge, cut, thrust, feint, so he knows some technique, which he'll need if I happen to be on holiday and he has to fight a dragon by himself. You see, being a hero when you've got a sword (not just a sword sword, but a demon sword like me) is a piece of cake. The sword does all the work. It pulls you around (providing you're not so fat that you can't move), it knows how to lead the dragon on, it knows how to confuse the stupid beast with techniques learned over millennia, and most importantly, it knows how to kill the dragon. Ah, you think that's an easy thing? Wait till you see the dragon…

And there it is.

It slithers right for us at maybe a hundred miles an hour, burrowing through the sand, sending it flying all over, and its breath is so hot that it turns the sand into glass all around it, leaving a trail of glass that reflects the sun like a mirror. It stops right in front of Harold and pulls itself up like a python to full height. Its scales look like precious stones, like blood-red rubies, but its head, which looks like the head of a huge fly, is covered with something that looks like layers and layers of puke and snot. If that stuff drips on you, you'll melt, I guarantee it. And its huge green eyes stare down at us as steadily as a crocodile watching its prey. It takes a deep breath and is about to turn everybody into barbecue.

"Harold, lift up your shield, dummy!"

Harold raises the shield as fire pours down

upon us, but that shield is pretty powerful stuff, and the dragon-flame breaks against the shield and turns into smoke and soot, so you probably can hardly see what's going on now. I leap into Harold's hand, and now you'll see what heroes are made of. Real heroes are the dummies. They hold the sword. It's the sword who does the fighting! But first I've got to get behind this stupid dragon, and maybe the dragon isn't so stupid because it's keeping its snotty, vomit-gooped head right in front of me. "Okay, Harold, remember what I taught you? Feint to the left, roll, keep that shield up or I'll be fighting the dragon alone—and watch it, it's dripping bile, you want to get us both melted?"

Okay, I should ask you something, even though we're right in the middle of fighting the dragon… even though all this green dragon-bile is falling all around us. (If enough of that stuff touches Harold—or me—it could dissolve us as easily as aspirin melts in water). So, listen up. Here's an easy question: If I'm doing all the fighting, why do I need a hero?

Because it's *traditional*, dummy!

And it gives you humans something to do!

Now that that's settled, back to the fight.

Oops, I warned you that dragons are dangerous. It feinted, swung its wormy neck around Harold and me, and turned everything to glass behind us.

"Okay, Harold, now's your chance. Run to the left quickly. I only need a second. There it is. See the spot right in the middle of the dragon's back. See the grey, wormy flesh where there's no scales. Jump! I got it, I'm burying myself right into its flesh. Yuk, I hate this part! Well, you can help pull me out of this damn dragon. Pull!

Okay, now back off because it's going to catch fire and—"

The damn thing explodes.

Fire shoots everywhere.

Dragon scales rip through the air like shrapnel.

Dragon-flesh drops into the sand like giant turds.

And it doesn't smell too pleasant either.

"Congratulations, Harold. One dragon bites the dust…er, the sand! Harold? Harold?"

Well, kid, this was his first time. He's allowed to pee in his armour and shake and snivel and cry.

The dragon is dead, so you can stop all that shaking and snivelling and crying too.

So your arm got burnt by a little bit of dragon bile. Big deal! Don't complain, you didn't even dissolve.

What a cry baby!

AND NOW FOR A HOLIDAY ON THE SUNNY ISLE OF THRINACIA

"Cry baby! Okay, you big five-foot-long lump of metal. That's enough. I've let you tell your version of how I became a hero. I bit my tongue at the ignominy of it all and didn't interrupt once, despite the obvious mendacities.

"Uh, oh, big words from the nerd."

"Now it's *your* turn to shut up and let me tell them *my* story, the one I started earlier before you interrupted."

The sword shimmered silently.

So, patient reader, this is the true story about how we went back in time; and before I go any further, I'm going to tell you right here and now (take a bow, Sword!) that the sword-maven is the one who knows how to do the time travel thing. That's one of his tricks that I haven't quite worked out yet. So from me you're just going to get a story. But what a story! I'm going to tell you how *I* singlehandedly saved that ancient Greek guy, Odysseus, from the one-eyed Cyclops—you should know about him from mythology and the movies—and I'm going to tell you about how this Cyclops was definitely going to dash Odysseus' brains out and eat him and everybody else who'd manned his rickety ship. And he also had me on the menu!

`"Well, he sure as hell wasn't going to eat me."`

"Shut up, sword!"

So, after we killed off that dragon in Göreme, I decided I really needed a holiday. "Remember that, Sword? You asked me where I wanted to go."

`"Of course, I remember! I never forget anything! I'm a demon, remember?"`

Anyway, reader, I told the sword I wanted to go to a Mediterranean island. Those islands are supposed to be really nice. You know, pleasant climate, great food, sandy beaches with warm, turquoise waters, cheap wine and a leisurely pace. (The cheap wine bit isn't in the tourist guides). Maybe Ibiza, Santorini or Mykonos, I thought.

`"So, Mr Putz who now calls himself a hero, what was your problem? I transported you to a Mediterranean island, just like you asked...or I should say begged."`

So the next thing you know, we found ourselves on the beach of a barren-looking island with a live volcano in the distance spurting burps of fire, smoke, and black ash. Picture this: on a hill just above us is a stand of tall oaks and pine trees, with a high wall of hewn rock around their base.

"This is your idea of a resort?" I asked.

`"Oh, look,"` the sword said, distracted. `"There's Odysseus."`

"Where in Hell are we?"

`"This isn't Hades; it's the Island of Thrinacia. The island of the Cyclopes."`

"What?"

`"Just follow those Greeks."`

73

And sure as rain after a red sunrise, a dozen or so men clad in ragged tunics and brandishing short swords were running up the beach. Odysseus's men, we figured. And they looked like they were half in the bag—

"**He means drunk.**"

—and three or four of them had enormous wine skins on their shoulders. By the time we caught up with them, they had passed through a gate in the wall of hewn rock and were detouring around a sheep pen littered with dung. We watched them slowly and cautiously enter the mouth of a large cave overgrown with laurel.

"What are we *doing* here, Sword?" I asked.

"Hunting for treasure, Harold."

"Treasure?"

"We've got to pay for this holiday somehow."

I won't go into why the sword thought this was a holiday. He can tell you about that on his own time. Swords have odd ideas of what constitutes a holiday. But, anyway, once we were inside the cave, I bumped right into the back of a stout Greek warrior. He was just standing there, awestruck.

The cave was enormous.

"Phew, it stinks like vomit," one of Odysseus's men said.

"It's the cheese," another said.

There were large wooden racks stacked with drying cheeses against the westernmost wall, and further along huge hand-hammered copper pails full of milk, curd, and whey sat in a row along a natural stone shelf.

"It's not the cheese," I said to the sword. "Can't they smell the dung? Ugh! The cave floor is covered in it. *That's* what stinks."

"I think you'll find the odour of dung is commonplace in these times."

"And how come I can understand what these guys are saying?"

The sword sighed…something he does a lot.

"**I do not!**"

Yeah, well, anyway, the sword's answer to my question was: "Because, Harold, I am a demon and have a surfeit of magical powers, which includes telepathy, invisibility, psychofamiliarity, and metamorphosis. So...would you rather I just stop translating? Then it will *all* be Greek to you." The sword chuckled.

It was my turn to sigh.

"Let's grab the cheeses and some of these sheep and goats and get out of here," said one of the Greeks.

"So where's this supposed treasure?" I asked the sword.

"Patience, Harold. It's here somewhere, I can *feel* it."

"You can feel it?"

"Isn't that what I just said?" the sword said... sighing yet again. I told you, he does that a lot.

Sigh!

One of Odysseus's men rekindled a fire that had been set in the centre of the cave, and they all sat down and started pouring wine and making a meal of the cheese. Their leader filled a carved wooden bowl with wine and a little water and passed it to me as if he'd known me for yonks. I took a sip. Actually, it wasn't bad. Strong, despite being watered, and a little heavy on the tannins; but not bad.

"Why haven't they recognised us as strangers?" I asked the sword, who sighed again because he can't make any facial expressions.

"You're pushing this sighing thing a bit far, hero!"

Okay, he's right...and I speak from experience, an angry sword is not a pretty sight! So to answer why the Greeks didn't ask who the hell we were, the sword said:

"I told you, I have the power of psychofamilarity. I've cast a glamour."

Then before the sword could say anything else, the cave suddenly went dim as the bulk of a giant filled the massive cave entrance.

"Intruders!" Its deep, booming voice echoed through the cave.

I caught a glimpse of its face in the flickering fire light; and I can tell you, it was ugly, very, very ugly. It could have been the love child of the winged monkeys and the Wicked Witch of the West. I could see it was a Cyclops because it had only one single glaring eye right in the middle of its forehead. (Just like the Purple People-Eater, if any of you are familiar with old pop songs).

"Who dares to invade my home?" it said. Read that as if it's in capital letters. I mean he was loud!

"We are men of Atrides Agamemnon on our way home from our great victory at Troy," the leader of the Greeks said. (That would be Odysseus himself).

"I smell a demon!" the Cyclops roared.

"Uh oh," whispered the sword.

"You cannot hide from me, Demon," the Cyclops roared, looking in our direction. Then he rolled a massive boulder into the entrance of the cave, blocking it securely. "I am Polyphemus, the *most* powerful of sorcerers, son of Poseidon the God of the Sea." (Again, think capital letters)!

I felt the sword tremble in my hand and knew we were in big trouble.

"I was not trembling; I was girding my loins."

Yeah, okay, Sword, you weren't trembling. To continue: Polyphemus' single eye began to glow with an eerie, sickly-green inner light and he said, "I bind you, demon!"

The sword became hot in my hands. So hot that I'm afraid I dropped it. It clanged as it hit the cave floor and began to glow dull-red.

"I am not an 'it', you little shit!"

Ignore that, reader.

So the sword began to melt and change form before my very eyes. Suddenly it was no longer a sword: it had become a large bronze pot.

"Ughh," the sword said. "I—I—I have—av—av lost—ost—ost my—y—y power—er—r"

"You are echoing," I said to him.

"Of course, I am echoing, you asshole—hole—hole. I have been transformed into a pot—ot—ot... A pisspot, of all things."

"Well, stop it, I can't understand you."

"I'll try," the sword said softly, this time no echo. "But the Cyclops has robbed me of my powers. It's a miracle I can even still speak."

I laughed a little. I couldn't help it.

Sigh!

Sorry, Sword. Okay, so meanwhile Odysseus and his men cowered in the rear of the cave. As if it wasn't enough that an enormous one-eyed giant had caught them pilfering his goods and would probably eat them for dinner, they stared at us in disbelief now that the sword's glamour had worn off.

"Uh, that young man and the, er, pisspot aren't with us," Odysseus said. "We, however, come as guests and supplicants in hope of a warm welcome and perhaps even the customary gift of hospitality from you, oh benevolent one. For Zeus who watches over us would be most displeased should any harm befall us."

The Cyclops let out a bellow of laughter. "I fear not Zeus, nor any of the other Gods of Olympus." With that the one-eyed giant lunged at the Greeks who huddled together around Odysseus, swept a pair of them up in his mighty fists and smashed their heads on the ground like unwanted kittens. Blood and brains splattered all over the dung on the floor and onto the feet of the remaining startled Greeks, who cringed and wept and cried out in terror.

Ignoring them, the Cyclops sat on a boulder that seemed shaped to fit his enormous gluteus maximus and began to tear the dead men limb from limb, eating them bloody and steaming, and smacking his thick rubbery lips in noisy pleasure with each mouthful. When he had finished his snack and nothing was left, no bones or guts or anything else save what might have been soaked up by the dung on the ground, he belched and gulped a bucket of raw milk to wash down his gory feast.

Then the giant stood up, flopped out his great penis, and pissed on the sword...I mean pissed into the bronze pot.

"Glub, glub, glub..."

"Hey," I said, "you didn't echo."

"Very funny," the transmogrified sword gurgled.

"Enough with the pissing! Get on with the story!"

Yeah, okay, so sated and relieved, the giant Cyclops shook some drops of urine from his penis. Then he sat down on the floor of the cave with his back against the wall and went right to sleep. Sleeping like a baby.

Except he didn't close his eye. The damn thing just stared into space. A big blue orb encased in yellow-whitish ichor. And before long the Cyclops was snoring so loud he sounded like a Mack truck revving its engine. But, as I said, his eye stayed open.

Then one of the Greeks crept towards him, but even as he slept the Cyclops saw the soldier and swatted him aside.

"Can he hear us?" Odysseus asked.

One of the men called to the giant: "Polyphemus?" The Cyclops didn't stir.

"Let's kill him," Odysseus said.

"Blub, glug, gurgle, splash," the sword/pisspot said.

"What did you say?" Odysseus asked. I figure at this point, Odysseus was used to giants and probably other various forms of weirdness, so a talking sword who'd just turned into a pisspot was no big deal.

"Empty me first and maybe I can help," the sword/pisspot said.

Although the pisspot was giant-sized, it was filled almost to the brim. It took the strength of three of Odysseus's men to overturn it. Piss spilled across the floor of the cave, pooling here and there, making the dung wet and sloppy and the fire sizzle. A rank smell filled the air.

"Thank—ank—ank the Gods," the now empty bronze pot said. "But even if you can kill him, how do you plan to move the massive stone from the entrance? Remember, the Cyclops who moves rocks like marbles will be dead."

I then had to explain to Odysseus and his men what marbles were.

Testing the sword/pot's words, the remaining ten men silently made their way to the stone—its bulk was on the outside of the cave, but had handholds chiselled into its inner surface so the

Cyclops could easily grip it—and tried to budge it. But they couldn't push it or lift it high enough for a bug to crawl under it.

"Won't you return to your demon form once the Cyclops is dead?" I asked the sword. "Won't your powers return?"

"Maybe, maybe not. I don't know, Harold. Do you want to risk being stuck in this dung-filled cave for the rest of what would be a very short life?"

It was now my time to save the day, so I said, "The only way we can escape is for my sword (who's been reduced to the status of pisspot) to get his power back."

Well, Polyphemus the giant Cyclops snored on, oblivious to all our strategies. Odysseus's men huddled unheroically together at the rear of the cave, moaning and waiting for dawn and a chance to escape.

"We have to find the source of Polyphemus's power," the sword said slowly, making a great effort not to echo. "And then it will be up to you to do whatever is necessary to unbind me, Harold. You want to be a hero. Then do a job!"

In the morning the Cyclops awakened, yawned, stood up, shook himself like a wet dog, and stretched. Then once again he emptied his bladder into the pot.

"Glub...glug...glub..." the sword gurgled in disgust.

I watched the giant closely as he milked his ewes and nanny goats and tried to discern the source of his sorcerous power but, frankly, I had no clue. When he finished, he left the lambs and kids to suckle what milk remained in their mothers' udders and hefted the massive stone aside from the mouth of cave. He picked it up with no more effort than you or I would pick up a pebble on the beach.

Sunlight flooded in, blinding me for an instant, just as one of Odysseus's men made a dash for the opening. Idiot! Polyphemus easily snatched him up, held him before that big blue eye in the centre of his forehead as if examining a strange, new bug, and then dashed his brains out against the rock wall and popped the limp corpse into his mouth. Another one of the men tried his luck, ducking behind the giant before making his run toward freedom. Although the Cyclops saw him, he couldn't move quickly enough to catch the young soldier-sailor who had just reached the mouth of the cave.

Terrible as it was to witness, I finally saw a way out of this mess. Well, I must admit, it didn't click in my mind immediately. But here's what happened:

The Cyclops grunted and his huge eye began to glow with that eerie inner light I'd mentioned before. It was a green ichorish colour. (Ichorish, not liquorice). And then, like a tractor beam from a *Star Wars* movie, the Cyclops's gaze froze the hapless absconder mid-stride. The poor bastard was caught like a fly in amber, and the Cyclops didn't waste any time before dashing his brains out against the wall and eating him. The crunching of bones and squishing of flesh was nauseating. Then, belching with contentment, he grabbed a large pail of curd, pushed the stone out of the way, shouldered his way out of the cave, and sealed the entrance securely behind him.

"Glub...gurgle...slosh... Somebody, anybody, help me, I'm drowning in p—"

"Empty him, empty the pisspot," I shouted. Odysseus and his remaining men wrestled with the pot until they finally overturned it. And, as the rank mossy odour of the Cyclops's piss filled the cave, it hit me (I don't even want to consider how I conflated Cyclops piss with glamour. Sigmund Freud would probably have something nasty to say about the strange and perverse connections my unconscious makes, but that would be his problem, not mine and nor would I care because me, my unconscious, and I found the answer): I told the sword/pisspot and Odysseus, "The source of the Cyclops's sorcerous power is his *eye!*"

A LITTLE MORE ABOUT THAT BIG BLUE CYCLOPEDIAN EYE

Since I'm admitting all sorts of things, I should mention that I was a bit bemused I could still understand what the Greeks were saying (in their ancient Greek—archaic Greek) and that they could still understand me, despite the sword having lost his demonic power. "How does that work?" I asked him.

"Beats me," said the sword. "I can only assume that Polyphemus is using his own version of telepathy and psychofamiliar translation which has us all speaking the same language."

"Why?"

The sword/pisspot sighed yet again. "Why? So he can converse with us, dummy!"

Anyway, we huddled together in the cave and made plans.

Well, actually, Odysseus broke out another one of his wine skins and filled a carved wooden bowl with the strong, acidic wine and a little water. The Greeks passed it around and proceeded to get drunk.

"You know, we could just get the Cyclops drunk," Odysseus said.

I shook my head. "No, we'll need to do more than that to stop him."

"You're right about that, hero," said the sword/pisspot. "When he returns, you'll have to take out his eye. That's your only chance."

Odysseus staggered off to take a piss (and *not* in the sword/pisspot) and found a great club of green olive-wood beside one of the sheep pens in the deepest part of the cave. It was as long as the mast of a twenty-oared galley. "We can lop off a length of this," he said, "shave it to a point with our swords, and char it to a hard stabbing point in the fire."

"But how will you heft it without the Cyclops seeing you?" I asked.

Odysseus's men muttered amongst themselves, but didn't seem to have any ideas. I look around the cave as if ideas would be lying around like coils of rope. In fact, I did spy a coil of rope. I also found rocks piled against the far wall; and as I walked around the cave taking what I think of as mind pictures, I also discovered that the cave's ceiling high above us was reinforced with thick oaken beams.

"I have an idea," I said and convinced them to set to work.

I should mention that it's not easy to get a bunch of half-drunk ancient Greek sailor-soldiers to do what you want. But after a lot of goading and prodding they eventually half-filled the sword— who was, of course, still in his pisspot embodiment—with rocks, tied him to one end of the rope (lucky that sailors know how to make good knots), and flung the other end over one of the thick ceiling beams.

"Now all we have to do," I said, "is pull the pisspot up to the ceiling of the cave and let go of the rope when the Cyclops steps underneath it."

"Oh, sure, easy-peasy," said the sword.

"Will it kill the Cyclops?" asked one of the men.

"If we are lucky—*very* lucky—it might knock him out. Or at least stun him so you, Odysseus, can stab him in the eye with that mighty stake."

"And what if it just makes him angry, Mr Big Brain?" The voice was rock-muffled.

Ignoring the sword/pisspot, Odysseus said, "That's all very well and good, but how are we supposed get the Cyclops to stand under the pot?"

"We'll need something to bait him."

Odysseus and all his men looked at me.

"Well," I said, "it looks like you might have enough booze to even get a Cyclops shitfaced."

"I had that idea earlier, and you naysayed it," said an irritated Odysseus.

"Yes, I did, great leader of men. But I am large, I contain multitudes."

Not having read Walt Whitman's *Song of Myself*, Odysseus

gave me a perplexed look and then nodded as if, indeed, he was a great fan of 19th century American poetry.

(As an ex-nerd, I do indeed know such things)!

AND NOW WE COME TO THE...CRUNCH

We heard the crunch of gravel and the grating of rock and were almost blinded by the flash of sunlight as Polyphemus entered the cave. The Cyclops looked around, grunted, and then moved the massive boulder back across the entrance. Once again, the cave was dimly lit. Shadows skittered across walls and ceiling; the fire popped and glowed, brightening, as Polyphemus's movement stirred the air like a bellows.

"You must be weary after your day's work," Odysseus said. "Why not sit for a while and relax." He poured a bowl of unwatered wine and offered it to the Cyclops. "Here, try some of our fine Attican wine as an offering to the great Polyphemus's puissant strength and divinity."

The one-eyed giant squinted suspiciously at Odysseus, accepted the bowl and sat down on his stone seat. He took a cautious sip, grunted with pleasure, and tossed the remainder back in a single gulp.

"More!" he demanded, holding out the empty bowl. "A good helping."

Odysseus refilled the bowl to the brim with the strong wine. The Cyclops swallowed it down and called for another. He quaffed that and insisted Odysseus refill it again. After three bowls he belched and got to his feet, staggering a little.

His voice slurred, he said, "I need food," and grabbed for one of the men. But missed, for the man manage to duck out of his way.

Polyphemus blinked his now glazed eye. "Hold still," he said. "My stomach is grumbling from lack of human flesh."

"Hey, you one-eyed git," I shouted, waving my arms to attract his drunken attention. "Hey, you fat, one-eyed, shit-smelling bastard seed of one of Poseidon's misguided trysts with some ogre whore. You should go on a diet. You look like an oversized basketball with a head."

Okay, I could hear the sword/pisspot mumble something about the Cyclops not having a clue about basketballs, so after an instant of reflection, I shouted, "You must get all that fat from your mother!" I gave him the finger and shouted, "Eat me!" I meant that in the derogatory streetwise sense. God forbid my journey would end as a bit of acid reflux in the stomach of this son of a god.

As I taunted the one-eyed smell of a fart, I walked backwards until I was right under the sword/pisspot who was filled with rocks and hanging under the ceiling. I could hear the heavy breathing of Odysseus's men who were crouched down behind one of the sheep pens as they strained to hold onto the rope.

The Cyclops stared down at me, and I could almost imagine a look of respect had crossed his pimply, jowly face. "So who are you, little pigmy, who dares to insult Polyphemus, the son of Poseidon?"

"My name? My name is... Nobody, that's my name," I said, thinking for some bizarre reason of Terrence Hill playing alongside Henry Fonda in the title role of a 1973 spaghetti western comedy. (And I don't even like spaghetti westerns)!

"That's your name?" the Cyclops asked, laughing. "Well, then, my little insect, then I will have Nobody for supper."

He hooted and lurched towards me. He was so drunk he almost fell over his own feet.

I bravely stood my ground.

"You were shaking in your boots!"

"Shut up! This is my story, Sword. And I wasn't wearing boots!"

Now, as I was saying, I stood my ground until Polyphemus was almost on top of me. I waited until he bent down to grab me before I screamed (which was our signal to act).

And as the men released their hold on the rope, as the sword/pisspot filled with rocks descended at a great rate of speed, I threw myself backward. That was all as it should be, but, unfortunately, one of the half-drunk Greeks had unwittingly left a dangling loop of rope on the floor of the cave, which, of course, I stepped into. As the pot came crashing down, the rope tightened around my ankles, and I found myself hauled feet-first up to the ceiling.

"**You screamed like a girl.**"

"Don't interrupt, Sword. I did no such thing!"

So there I was, hanging upside-down above the Cyclops; and far from being knocked out, Polyphemus was bellowing like a bull undergoing castration. Yet drunk and knocked almost senseless, the enraged Cyclops managed to grab another one of Odysseus's men and dash his brains out.

"You're next," he said to Odysseus.

"Oh, shit," Odysseus moaned, which, if you need a translation is "Ω, σκατά!" Sounds sort of like *omega kata*. (I just thought you'd like to hear Odysseus swearing in the original tongue, dear reader).

While all this was going on, I managed to loosen the rope around my feet, only to fall right onto Polyphemus's pustuled nose, which, I can tell you, was as slippery as an egg on glass. I reflexively grabbed his eyelid—it was the size of a roller blind—to balance myself; and in so doing, my weight pulled his eye shut.

Polyphemus tossed his head from side to side and roared in fury, but I held on like a fly on glass…to continue my continuing metaphor.

I heard Odysseus shout, "Look! Treasure!"

And as I was being whipped about like a pennant in a gale—yes, I know, mixing metaphors—I held onto Polyphemus's eyelid for my life. Everything seemed to tumble around me, as if I was caught in some giant, poorly-lit kaleidoscope. I caught glimpses of glittering objects: was that a jewel-encrusted gold chalice sitting on a shelf where a wooden bowl had been? Wasn't that mound of jewels catching the firelight once a pile of rocks? And weren't those ingots of silver and gold formerly stacks of cheeses?

"Hold on, Harold," shouted the sword; and, indeed,

Sword was no longer a pisspot. As long as I was pulling down the Cyclops's eyelid, essentially blinding him, Polyphemus's powerful glamour was interrupted.

"We've got to put his eye out immediately!"

Polyphemus swatted at me, as if I were the aforementioned proverbial fly, and caught me with a glancing blow, which stunned me. One of my hands lost its grip on his eyelid, but I held on for dear life with my other hand; and before the Cyclops could pluck me from his face and squash me into an unwilling hamburger patty, something cold and hard thumped into the palm of my free hand.

A familiar voice: "We can do this, Harold."

I recognised the familiar feel of the hilt of the sword who is called THE-GLORIOUS-SWORD-OF-FIRE-AND-DESTINY-THAT-BURNS-AND-CUTS-THROUGH-FLESH, and even as I lost my grip on Polyphemus's giant eyelid, I simultaneously plunged the sword deep into the Cyclops' eye.

Sticky blood and gore exploded all over the sword and me. The Cyclops screamed so loud it could be felt as vibration. And then I was falling, and I, too, was shouting, the last triumphal shout of a hero; and I didn't let go of the sword. My skull might be crushed in the fall, but I would not lose my sword.

Heroes don't lose their swords!

And as I fell, the sword, seemingly unperturbed by the idea that I had escaped being crushed into a hamburger patty, only to be flattened into a pancake, said, "That was close. A split second more and you would have merely bumped him in the eye with a pisspot."

IT AIN'T OVER YET

I was covered in stinking, steaming gore. Everything smelled like shit, probably because I had just landed in a thick, wet clump of straw and stinking dung.

"That's lucky," the sword said. "It broke your fall."

"Thanks for your kind consideration."

But Polyphemus was still very much alive and active: he blundered blindly around the cave, shrieking and bellowing, smashing and breaking anything and everything in his path. He caught another one of Odysseus's men and bashed his brains out. All the while, would you believe, it was Polyphemus who was crying for help; and I've got to tell you, for a moment, I thought Poseidon himself had heard his pleas and had come to his aid. The ground shook as if an earthquake had erupted all around us. Well, to cut to the chase, it wasn't Poseidon: it was the neighbouring Cyclopes who lived in the many other caves on the nearby windswept crags.

"What is wrong, brother?" they shouted. "Is somebody trying to kill you?"

"Nobody is trying to kill me," Polyphemus roared.

"If nobody is trying to kill you," they shouted, "then you should pray to your father Poseidon. Zeus must be to blame for whatever ails you."

"*Nobody* has blinded me and is trying to kill me!"

After that pronouncement, the other Cyclopes left (as far as they were concerned, it was in the hands of the Gods; after all, Cyclopes aren't the most fraternal and sensitive of species), and the eyeless Polyphemus groped his way to the mouth of the cave and rolled back the stone. Too late he realised his mistake, for Odysseus and his four remaining men bolted through the opening and ran for the beach as quick as they could, leaving me and my trusty sword behind.

"I was not, am not, and will never ever be your trusty sword, nerd-boy!"

"Sorry, Sword, don't get hot under your, er, hilt."

So, readers, allow me to continue the story, which is, alas, almost at an end. As you might have guessed, the Cyclops chased after Odysseus and his men, following the sound of their running feet; and we were left on our own in the quietude of his stinking, treasure-filled cave. I sheathed Sword and made my way over to the golden jewelled chalice. It was exquisite. Wrought by a master craftsman. I picked it up. It felt surprisingly warm.

"Leave that, oh greedy one," the sword said. "You can grab anything else you can carry, but that chalice is destined for another kind of hero living in another time. But hurry, whatever you do, because we don't have much time."

I reluctantly replaced the chalice and decided to collect the gold ingots; but they were just too damn heavy, like lumps of lead. Who knew gold weighed so much? Even for a muscle-bound hero like me. So I came to my senses and stuffed fistfuls of diamonds, rubies, emeralds and sapphires into a muslin bag the Cyclops used to squeeze out the liquid whey from the cheese curd. The gems, too, were heavy as hell, but I thought of flag and country and shouldered my hard burden.

BUT NOW THE END IS NEAR

Standing on a rocky crag, I looked down onto the beach. Odysseus and his men had already boarded their waiting ship and the crew who had remained on board to guard the vessel and keep it ready for a quick getaway cast off. The oarsmen churned the water with each strong, synchronised stroke and in response the ship pulled quickly away. But Odysseus, ah, Odysseus, he couldn't control his pride. He was the living embodiment of hubris. We—Sword and I—watched him make his way over to the stern to shout, "How dare you eat your honoured guests, Polyphemus, you shithead."

The Cyclops roared in exasperation.

"Did I not warn you, you one-eyed and now no-eyed loser, that I am under the protection of Zeus? Remember me, Polyphemus, remember my name, for I am Odysseus, King of Ithaca!"

"Fool," the sword muttered. "He's a braggart and a fool. Zeus couldn't give one small shit about Odysseus. But Poseidon...now there's a god who knows how to hold a grudge."

The blind Polyphemus tore a gigantic chunk of rock away from the headland and hurled it in the direction of Odysseus's voice. It splashed into the sea just ahead of the ship, creating a mighty wave that washed the ship back towards shore.

"Row!" Odysseus shouted to his men. "Row for your lives!"

"Will they escape?" I asked the all-knowing sword.

"That's more like it, hero."

And the sword challenged me: "Haven't you read your Homer, Harold?"

I responded with my usual sense of certainty: "Well, umm….."

"Never mind," said the sword. "Homer got it all wrong anyway. But it wasn't his fault."

"So do they make it home?"

"Yes, eventually. But it will take them years and years. Because Odysseus couldn't leave well enough alone and had to be the big shot, Polyphemus will call to his father to extract revenge, and Poseidon will… Ach, Mr Hero. Go read the damn book!"

And that, friends, is the true story about how I, Harold the Hero, singlehandedly (well, okay, maybe the sword helped out a little) saved Odysseus and (some) of his men. Not to mention saving the Talking Sword. And that's how I escaped with enough treasure to have a *real* Mediterranean island holiday. In fact, I now have enough to buy myself an entire island.

Anything you want to add, Sword?

VIDEO GAMES ANYONE: A LAST WORD

Yes, thank you. This last little bit is known as the denouement. The final outcome. This is where I wrap everything up so we can all go home.

Harold doesn't shake and pee in his armour anymore when we have to fight a dragon. In fact, as you might have noticed, he has got a bit of a big head and thinks he's without flaw—

"That's not true!"

—but at least he hasn't fallen in love with a damsel in distress (yet).

However, a little bird told me that Harold the Hero will soon be heading off on his own for a— well, for another—well-earned holiday. And I have that certain feeling that he might just meet an undistressed damsel. And we can all extrapolate what might happen then: he would give up the hero business. Just like that. Which would be a shame because we really do make a great team.

Just ask Odysseus.

So what will *I* do if Harold finds true storybook love?

Oh, I suppose I could get myself a new hero.

But, you know what I've been thinking about a lot lately?

I might just take a break and go into video game programming. I could design some mean video games. How about something like a game called *The Talking Sword*?

Why not, hey?

And I've had my eye on one of those whiz-bang smart phones for a while. I might even buy myself a new Jag.

Of course, I'd have to grow some arms and hands. But that's no problem.

I'm a demon, after all...

Harold the Hero and the Talking Sword — Afterword

Jack Dann and I had been talking for a while about doing a project together when the opportunity to write a story for Clan Destine Press' *And Then...* anthology came up. He showed his story 'The Talking Sword' to Lindy Cameron and she loved it, but suggested it be expanded because the theme of the anthology was for stories with two protagonists, and the demon sword held sway over his "sidekick" in Jack's original tale.

As Jack and I talked about it, we soon found ourselves brainstorming the further adventures of not just the time-travelling sword, but having his unlikely wielder, Harold the Hero, come to the fore. We took our inspiration from Homer's *Odyssey*, and asked ourselves what would happen if the sword somehow lost its powers. The result was 'Harold the Hero and the Talking Sword'. It was great fun to write and hopefully it's great fun to read.

Fixed in Time

"Congratulations, Patrick," Dr Singh said. "You are officially dry."

"*Again*," I said. *But would I stay dry,* I wondered? The booze still whispered to me with its silver tongue, called my name.

I looked down at the grey vinyl floor between my feet.

There was a moment of silence.

I sat on the bed in my small rehab clinic room. Dr Singh sat opposite me on the moulded-plastic visitor chair. On his lap he held a fat manila folder stuffed with documents.

"I see you've been drawing again." He stood up, put the manila folder on the chair, and went over to leaf through the pile of sketches on the desk in the corner. "These are very good. You have quite a talent."

"Not enough to make a bloody living."

"Perhaps if you chose different subjects. Always the girl and the house."

I shrugged.

"Your childhood friend."

"Yeah."

"The incident with her happened fifteen years ago, Patrick. When will you stop blaming yourself? You were only a child of ten. It's time for you to put all this behind you and move on with your life. I can help you do that."

I chewed at my thumbnail.

He held up a pencil sketch and examined it. It was a good one. I had captured the childlike sparkle in her eyes. The hint of a mischievous smile at the corner of her mouth.

"Patrick, last time we spoke, you stopped your story when Mary reached the door of the house. Can you tell me what happened after that?"

I shook my head. I had stopped telling people years before. Nobody ever believed me. The bastards all thought I was crazy.

"Give it a try," he said gently.

I clenched my fists and opened my mouth to reply, but nothing came out.

He nodded encouragement.

I took a deep breath. "The abandoned house was near my primary school. All the kids reckoned the house was haunted. It gave me the creeps so I always ran past it. Mary used to laugh at me, the way kids do."

Dr Singh selected another sketch from the pile. "This house?"

It was not as good as the one of Mary. I had scribbled it in biro in the midst of my withdrawal and it was full of anger and minimalistic sharp lines. Nevertheless, it captured the basics of the house: double storey, gable windows in a high-pitched roof, a front veranda.

"What happened?" he asked.

"One day Mary went into the house."

I squirmed. My head was throbbing and I started to sweat. I would have given anything for a bloody drink.

"You can trust me, Patrick."

I pursed my lips and steeled myself. I supposed he was right. If I couldn't trust him after all this time, who could I trust?

I sighed. "I didn't want to go in but I couldn't leave her there alone. So I ran after her. By the time I got to the front door she'd already gone inside and started up the staircase."

I remembered the expression on her face when she glanced at me. The determination, the recklessness in her eyes.

Dr Singh put the picture back on the desk, crossed the room, picked up the manila folder and sat back down on the visitor chair. "Go on," he said.

"I followed her but something was impeding me, making every step an effort, like I was trying to wade across a river.

Mary paused at the top of the stairs, peering along the hallway there, but I couldn't see her properly. She seemed somehow to be wavering, insubstantial."

I closed my eyes and saw her again across the years, remembered pushing up the stairs towards her, the struggle of each step physically painful, until only a couple of paces separated us.

"Patrick?" Dr Singh said.

It was cold, icy cold. I was shivering, though I still don't know to this day if it was from the cold or the fear.

He touched me on the knee. "Patrick."

I opened my eyes and looked at him. "By the time I reached the landing," I said, "Mary was already moving along the hallway. Then suddenly the house seemed to warp and distort. I felt dizzy. I thought I'd throw up."

Dr Singh leaned in closer. "What do you mean, the house warped and distorted?"

How much should I tell him? I wondered. What if he decided I *was* crazy? But he had been my shrink for three years and he hadn't sectioned me yet.

I went to the desk, riffling through my sketches until I found the one I was looking for. I held it up for him to see. "Like this. Like someone grabbed hold of the damned house and twisted it."

He took the picture of the misshaped hallway from me as I sat back on the bed. He arched an eyebrow.

The floor was tilted, the hallway curved, and the angles were wrong. The tall grandfather clock against the wall was bending forward, its face peering down, the way it *looked* at Mary.

"What happened next?" he asked.

"There was an open door at the end of the hall. A blinding white light shone out from it." In my mind's eye I could still see Mary standing frozen, silhouetted. "The tick of the clock began to get louder and louder."

"What did Mary do?"

"She just stood there. I tried to call out to her, but my voice was little more than a hoarse croak."

Her short, sharp breaths came out in small puffs of cloud.

"I reached out to her, but it was like putting my hands into a bloody freezer. The cold air rasped at my throat, like I was breathing razor blades."

By then each tick of the clock was like a clap of thunder. I tried to lunge for her but I couldn't move, I was fixed in time like a statue. Then the grandfather clock struck the hour.

GONG... GONG... GONG...

It seemed to go on forever.

The sound still gives me goose bumps.

"Then it all turned to shit."

I choked back a sob.

Dr Singh handed me a box of tissues. "What happened?"

I snatched some tissues and wiped the tears welling in my eyes. Then I met his gaze and he nodded for me to continue.

"Mary screamed. Then she vomited blood. It gushed bright red down her chin, all down the front of her school tunic. She cupped her hands and the blood steamed as it spilled over them."

I broke into deep, shuddering sobs.

Dr Singh took control. He consoled me with cool professional efficiency and waited until my tears subsided and my breathing started to return to normal.

"Can I get you a glass of water or a cup of tea?"

I blew my nose on a couple of tissues.

That memory, that bloody image of Mary has haunted my dreams, my nightmares, for the last decade. I can still smell her blood, sweet and coppery.

"I'm sorry, Patrick. I know this is painful for you. But in order to help you I have to ask, what happened next?"

I leaned forward, clasped my head in my hands and looked at the floor. At the blandness of the vinyl, at the grubby laces in my running shoes. After a few moments I took a deep breath, sat up, and continued.

"There's not much more to tell. Before I could do anything the hallway twisted again. A bitterly cold wind howled in from nowhere, lifted Mary from her feet and blew her away from me into the room."

The wind cut through me, like driven icicles. But despite its Arctic power the wind only took Mary.

"The door to the room slammed shut and the hallway went dark. Then something thumped me in the chest. Something hard and solid."

I wiped away the tears that ran unbidden down my cheeks and looked away.

Dr Singh waited in anticipation.

I picked at my fingernails. "I woke up in hospital. The police found me unconscious at the foot of the stairs. They called an ambulance. I had concussion, broken ribs, and a broken leg."

"Mary?"

"She was gone."

I looked squarely at Dr Singh and inspected his face, looking for any sign of a smile or a sneer. But his expression was open, guileless.

"There's no mention of any blood at the scene on the police report," he said.

I shrugged.

"Do you blame yourself for what happened to her?"

"Mary's parents blamed me. They came to see me in the hospital. They didn't believe me when I told them what happened. Her mother said I was a liar. When I came out of hospital me and my family moved away. I've never been back."

Dr Singh opened the manila folder on his lap, flicked through the papers and paused to read one. "Well the police said she was probably abducted by a person, or persons, unknown who pushed you down the stairs. I think that sounds like the more logical explanation, don't you?"

Great, I thought, *he doesn't believe me either.* I know it's a hard story to accept and sometimes I hardly believe it myself, because I can't help wondering, what if everyone else is right? Maybe it was all just a story I made up when I was a kid.

"It also said the blow to your head, the trauma of what you witnessed, made you block out the real events and create a fantasy to explain what had happened."

I should never have opened my mouth, I thought. *He's just like everyone else.*

Dr Singh studied me thoughtfully. "I think you are telling the truth, Patrick. Or at least your version of the truth. Something strange did happen in that house."

My heart began to race. Did he really mean that? A wave of relief washed over me.

"It might be helpful for you to go back there as part of your therapy."

I lurched back. "Are you for fucking real?"

He nodded.

"No bloody way."

"It's perfectly normal to be scared, but I will go there with you. If it gets too much, we will come straight back here."

What if I'm wrong? I thought. *What if the house isn't there? But will he believe my story if the house is still there?* I drummed my fingers on my knees.

Fuck, I need a drink. Any gut-rot will do.

He rose to his feet and took me by the hand. "Come on, let's give it a try. We can be back by lunch."

I stood up and followed meekly. I had always found it hard to say no to Dr Singh, and he was probably right. If I was ever going to make a real life for myself I had to confront the fear, but I didn't like this at all.

Dr Singh showed me to his car and we set off.

It was okay at first, but as the streets and suburbs flashed by I began to squirm in my seat. Beads of perspiration broke out on my forehead. "I'm not sure this is a good idea," I said.

"We are almost there," Dr Singh said.

The car's GPS navigated us to the street where it had happened. He parked and we got out and looked around. The school was gone, replaced by a housing estate. Just one of the many baby boomer schools that popped up for a decade or so, when almost every house in the area rang with the shouts and laughter of children.

We walked along the footpath to where I remembered the house had been. I was trembling, sick to my stomach.

Dr Singh tried to counsel me with calming words.

"That's the house," I said when we reached the spot, but I couldn't bring myself to look directly at it. Other things in the neighbourhood had changed, but not the house. I could still feel it.

"Goodness," Dr Singh said. "I see what you mean. It is a creepy sort of place; it almost feels like it's watching us. It's run down, just like in your drawings. The yard is overgrown and there's no sign of life."

I looked at my watch. It was almost eleven. I felt chilled to my soul.

"Let's get the hell out of here," I said.

"Hold on, you're just getting anxious, Patrick. Breathe like I showed you. In, one-two. Hold, one-two. Out, one-two."

I breathed like he told me and steadied myself. Then I glanced at the house, up at the gable windows.

I gasped. "It's Mary, there she is."

He clasped my shoulder in a firm grip. "It's natural to have a hallucination after what you have been through."

"No! Up there. In the window."

I followed his gaze as he looked up.

Mary was staring down at us. Still ten years old, with bright red blood running down her chin, all down the front of her.

I turned to Dr Singh. His face crumbled.

"Dear God," he said.

Somewhere in the distance I heard a clock striking the hour.

Mary placed her bloody palms against the window pane. Red rivulets dribbled down the glass.

I started to run up the path to the house, but Dr Singh moved quicker and grabbed my arm.

"No," he yelled. "The house will get you too."

"I told you it was true," I cried. I started to laugh, and couldn't seem to stop.

Dr Singh pulled me away, dragging me along with him.

I struggled to pull free.

"Stop it, Patrick. Are you crazy? You can't go in there."

I stopped laughing. "No, Dr Singh. I'm not crazy. I am vindicated."

Then there was a sound from the house, the complaining of old timbers moving against their will.

We spun around.

Mary was beckoning to us with her finger.

Dr Singh released his grip on me and stared at her as if in a trance. Then he started up the overgrown path towards the veranda steps.

I lunged for him, but he swatted me aside with unexpected force and I stumbled and fell to the ground.

As he reached the house the front door swung open with a creak.

Fixed in Time — Afterword

When I was a child we had to walk down a long, narrow lane to reach our primary school. A version of the house in this story really existed on the corner of that lane. The house had been empty and derelict for as long as I could remember, and rumours of murder and ghosts abounded in the schoolyard. Once, when I was about seven or eight years old, I went up the path and looked in the open front door…and then ran away.

It was a scary place.

But the house may not be the only culprit here.

Perhaps Phil is more than an observer. I can't help wondering if he has some sort of connection to the building and his *being there* somehow enables or breathes life—so to speak—into the house…

This story is original to the collection.

The Place

Somewhere deep, dark, and silent, Cudgewa slept with many others of his kind… Until hunger began to disturb his rest, its pangs stirring him. Had he physical form, one could say he yawned and stretched, but when Cudgewa sleeps he has no form save a quiescent awareness. Nevertheless, in that moment of restlessness, he reached out, more asleep than awake, to the Place of Plenty.

Jason Bird cursed as the new white Ford in front braked unexpectedly. He swerved his car out of the right lane and into the left one. He wiped sweat from his brow and scowled at the offending driver as he came alongside, but the man paid him no heed, staring straight ahead as cool as you like.

What a jerk, thought Jason and gave him the middle finger "highway salute".

The other driver looked like a business manager in his dark suit jacket, white shirt, and neatly knotted necktie. Jason tugged uncomfortably at his own already loosened collar and felt a trickle of perspiration run down his chest. He wrinkled his nose as he caught a whiff of his own rank underarm perspiration.

The inside of the car felt like an oven.

"Fuckin' air conditioner!" he said, twisting the knob on the dashboard in a vain attempt to coax the broken system back to life. But the only air coming from the vent was hot, hotter even than when the thing was on heat in the winter.

He pressed down hard on the accelerator and roared ahead of the man in the Ford.

A wave of nausea and dizziness washed over him in a hot flush. For a brief moment he lost control of the car, then the weird feeling passed as quickly as it had come, and he swerved back on course.

Must be the damned heat, he thought, shaking his head.

The street where he lived with his wife and children was coming up on the right. He glanced in his rear view mirror as he prepared to change lanes, only to do a double take.

The new white Ford in the right lane was overtaking him. Normally he would have just waited for it to pass, but this time Jason calmly and deliberately veered his car into its path then slammed on his brakes. He heard the screech of tyres and saw the Ford swerve and skid out of control, its business-suited driver throwing his arms over his wide eyes as his vehicle careened into a lamp post with a tremendous crash.

Over his shoulder, Jason saw the driver's head punch a bloody hole in the windscreen. He smiled.

The man obviously had not been wearing his seatbelt.

Jason's smile turned into a grin.

He had enjoyed it.

Calmly he switched on his indicator and turned into his street. As he pulled into his driveway he could hear a siren in the distance. Jason's ten-year-old son, Peter, let him into the house.

"Hi, Dad." The grinning boy took his father's briefcase. "I got ten out of ten in my maths test today."

Jason walked into the kitchen, leaving Peter standing at the door as though the boy did not exist.

"You're late, I was worried." Helen, Jason's wife, gave him a fleeting kiss on the cheek as she turned from the kitchen bench with a glass of water in her hand.

"I caused a car wreck," Jason said.

"Here's your drink, Gloria," Helen said, hearing but not

registering his words. "Come on, come and get it, I haven't got all day. Dinner's nearly ready."

A slight, dark-haired girl appeared, grabbed the glass and plonked herself back in front of the television in the family room.

"It's too hot to cook, Jay," Helen said as she went back to slicing tomato, "so we're having cold cuts and salad okay? Last night's leftover roast beef." She handed him the carving knife and fork. "Will you carve the meat? It's on the bench under the dish towel."

Jason stood before his wife with the carving utensils in his hands. He gazed from the fork to the knife and back again.

"Over there," she said, waving a lettuce leaf at the roast.

Jason looked at the long tines on the fork, then stared into his wife's face. In one swift, deliberate motion he drove the implement into her left eye, penetrating her brain. She died instantly, crumpling with hardly a sound. Blood and other fluids oozing from her eye socket.

In the kitchen doorway, their son Peter had witnessed the brutal slaying. He convulsed—trying to scream and gasp at the same time. Smiling, Jason turned from his wife's inert body. He laughed aloud when he saw the boy. He leapt at him, slashing rabidly with the carving knife. Peter went down, screaming at last, as his life spilled onto the hall carpet.

Brought from the television by her brother's screams, Gloria could not comprehend what had happened. She shrieked and burst into tears, running to her father's arms. Jason held her for a moment, grinning wickedly. Then he found her neck and clenched his hands around it. Gloria dangled at arm's length— kicking, twitching, a hollow gurgling sound escaping from her lips. When she was still, Jason dropped her to the floor beside her brother.

The smile on Jason's face disappeared, replaced by a bewildered expression. He felt ill, dizzy, as though he were about pass out. He felt hot. He closed his eyes and held them shut, then shook his head and opened them. His mind reeled as he saw his children at his feet and the recollection and realisation of what he had done came to him. A bitter, hot taste rose in his throat and he vomited bile.

Wiping muck and spittle from his lips he rushed into his bedroom, sobbing, fumbling with the bedside table drawer as he withdrew the loaded .38 Special he kept there for home defence and placed the barrel in his mouth...

Cudgewa yawned and rolled over, so to speak, and returned to sleep, his hunger satisfied for the moment. He slept peacefully, dreaming of the time of feasting—looking forward to the moment when he and all his kind would awaken together and go back to the Place of Plenty to gorge themselves.

The Place — Afterword

This story distressed me when I wrote it and still makes me uncomfortable today. So why did I write it? I wrote it in response to a spate of family murder-suicides and child murders that were reported in the news that shook me to the core. What drives a mother to drown her babies? Why would a father throw his daughter off a bridge? I don't understand how any parent can kill a child. There is no possible reason or excuse. Mental illness, I hear some people say. It makes me want to weep, so I guess this story was an attempt to exorcise the pain.

'The Place' was published in the very first edition of *Terror Australis* magazine.

The Wine Cellar

Sue folded her arms tightly against her chest and turned away from Rick to stare out the dark-tinted window of the limousine. The sleek black car pulled away from the Melbourne airport arrivals zone. The air conditioner blew cool air against her flushed cheeks.

"What's wrong?" Rick asked.

She sighed and scowled at him. "This was supposed to be special. A romantic week alone together by the sea."

"It *is* special. What do you call this chauffeur-driven limo?" He gestured to a compact bar subtly illuminated with blue LED lights. "Look, there's even French bubbly."

"It's lovely, Rick." She had to admit it was a nice touch. "But I wanted to stay in Portsea or Barwon Heads, not Belgrave. It sounds like a cemetery. And I wanted to be alone with you, not playing hostess to your friends."

He reached out and gently took her hand in his. "Phil and Linda aren't coming until the weekend. We'll have plenty of time together before they arrive."

She pulled free of his grasp, refolded her arms and crossed her legs.

"C'mon, babe. Relax. You've been working too hard. Was it a bad flight? Are you tired?"

"Don't call me babe."

"C'mon, Sue."

"Of course I'm tired, Rick. Yes, I've been working hard. We haven't seen each other for weeks. I wanted us to have a resort holiday, to be pampered, not to stay free in your cousin's weekend shack."

"He's my second cousin, Vincent."

She rolled her eyes. "I don't care if he's your third cousin twice removed."

"Trust me, Sue. Wait 'til you see the place." He squeezed her arm. "Let me fix you a drink."

He set out two crystal champagne flutes on the small bar, and removed a half bottle of *Moet et Chandon* from the silver ice bucket. He wiped the bottle dry with a crisp, white linen napkin and popped the cork.

As she watched Rick pour the sparkling wine, Sue could not help admiring his ruggedly handsome face, his alluring blue eyes, his easy, slightly lop-sided smile. He was right, of course, she should try to relax. All she had wanted for weeks, months, was to be with him. She thought he might be "the one". She wanted more than anything for him to pop the question...or at least raise the topic. Otherwise it would be up to her.

They had met about a year ago at an IT conference on the Gold Coast, and she had fallen for him. He had added a new dimension to her life. Wining and dining, parties, fun friends. And tenderness—Rick was an attentive, caring lover. But she worked in Brisbane and he worked in Melbourne, so they tried to grab time together when they could. A long weekend here, some annual leave there.

It was a hell of a way to have a relationship.

She accepted the glass, observing the long trains of tiny bubbles rising to the top. The champagne was her favourite. That was something else he had taught her: how to appreciate good wine. Screw it, she thought. A week with him anywhere was better than being alone in Brisbane.

They clinked glasses.

"To you, babe," he said.

He was teasing her and she grimaced at his jibe. "To a wonderful romantic week together, Rick."

"This is it," Rick announced, as the limousine glided to a halt. They had passed through the township of Belgrave, taken a winding road shaded by tree ferns and towering mountain ash trees. Then they had turned down a dirt track that meandered through thick bushland, eventually leading them to the house belonging to Rick's second cousin.

Sue gasped as it came into view. The house was charming. Not some fibro-cement shack after all, but a white-painted weatherboard Federation-style house with a slate roof and wide veranda. It seemed to be built into a hill, surrounded at the front and sides with tree ferns as big as beach umbrellas and enormous hydrangea bushes studded with bright blue cauliflower-sized blooms.

"Okay," she said. "The outside looks good but I'll have to see the inside before I let you off the hook."

Rick grinned. "I've seen photos. It's completely authentic. Original decor and antiques. Apparently my great uncle built it, but I never met him. In fact, I hardly know Vincent. He inherited it after his parents died and had it modernised, of course: new wiring, plumbing, all mod cons. But the silly bugger never uses it. Lucky if he's been up here twice in the last eighteen months."

"Then it'll probably be full of spiders and snakes. I'm not staying if it's not up to scratch."

He laughed. "Nah, the housekeeper and gardener come every month. But do you want to know the best thing about it?"

"The fact that we're miles from anywhere and nobody will disturb us? Oh, wait. Except for your friends, Phil and Linda, that is. And why are they coming anyway, Rick? You haven't explained that yet."

"They're coming because of the Wine Appreciation Society."

Sue snorted.

The Wine Appreciation Society had only four members: Rick, Phil, Linda, and herself. They had invented it after a boozy dinner party one night when they were all sozzled, and swore allegiance to the grape, to the pursuit of fine wines.

"You've got to be friggin' joking."

"Phil insisted. He wouldn't take no for an answer."

"Why?" She raised an eyebrow to let him know it better be good.

Rick dangled a key. "The wine cellar."

"The wine cellar?"

"That's what I've been trying to tell you. Seems my great uncle was a wine buff, but my second cousin hates the stuff. He's a beer and spirits man. He says the cellar is chock-a-block with old bottles. Told me we could help ourselves. Can you believe it?"

"Why would Vincent lend you the place if you hardly know each other? Let alone give us the run of the wine cellar. Surely he knows the vino might be valuable?"

"We met at a family reunion and got talking over a few drinks. He seemed like a nice guy and he just offered the place to us."

"Then you had to go and brag about the wine cellar to Phil."

Rick's face coloured a little. "I couldn't resist. Wine is my religion." He rubbed his hands in gleeful anticipation. "I can't wait to see what's down there."

"It'll be just our luck to find it's all gone off."

"Doubt it. Vincent said his grandpa excavated the cellar into the hillside. The old man was half Italian and half French. Had a taste for red wine before the Aussie palate had matured much beyond Barossa Pearl and Pink Starwine. Perfect conditions down there, I reckon."

As the limousine pulled away from the house, Rick dropped their bags in the hallway and kicked the front door shut. Sue put the esky he had brought on the floor beside them. Then he took her in his arms and kissed her tenderly. A warm glow spread through her. She breathed in his scent and her pulse raced.

Finally, they broke free.

Rick grinned. "I love you."

She kissed him lightly on the cheek and turned, smiling, to look at herself in the mirror of the tall mahogany hall stand beside them. Her face was flushed, her hair mussed. As she ran her fingers through her hair, she couldn't help admiring the antique hall stand with its carved scrollwork and brass hat pegs. It even had hooped umbrella holders on either side, with an umbrella in one and an old walking stick in the other.

Rick took a worn grey felt fedora with a band of black ribbon off one of the pegs and put it rakishly on his head. "Here's lookin' at you, kid," he said in a bad Humphrey Bogart imitation.

Sue followed him, hat and all, on a whirlwind tour of the house. There were polished Baltic pine floors, Persian rugs, cast iron fireplaces, and decorative plasterwork; it was appointed like the blurb in a brochure for a boutique hotel. And the furniture! She loved the intricately carved walnut dining table and cabriole leg chairs, the dark leather Chesterfield couch, and the red velvet *chaise longue*.

She paused in the lounge room and sat down on the Chesterfield. "This is a gorgeous house, Rick. I don't understand why Vincent doesn't come to the place more often."

"I think the place reminds him of his grandmother. Apparently she disappeared here."

"Disappeared?" Sue shivered involuntarily. "What happened?"

"He was vague about it. Reckons she must have wandered off into the bush and got lost. She was never found."

Sue got up and crossed to the fireplace. On the mantel was a framed black and white photograph of an elderly couple sitting together in this very room. She took it down and moved over to the window where the light was better. "This must be the grandparents."

He joined her to examine the picture. "Yeah, I reckon. Enzo and Florence were their names. Look, the old boy is wearing the same hat I am. He went funny after she disappeared."

She studied them. Enzo was sitting forward with his hands folded on top of a walking stick, staring straight into the camera. Florence was sitting primly with her hands clasped on her lap. Sue did not like the look of the old man. "Funny how?"

"A nervous breakdown or something. Grief. Vincent said he

used to rave on and on that something had taken her."

"What do you mean? Like an animal?"

Rick shrugged.

"What happened to him?"

"They had to put him in a home. He must have been depressed because he killed himself."

"Here?" she said in alarm.

"No, in the asylum or sanatorium or whatever they called it back then." He gave a wry, sad smile and doffed the hat. "There are no skeletons in the closet here. C'mon," he said, moving on down the hall to continue the tour.

Sue crossed to the fireplace to put the picture frame back on the mantel. She studied the photograph as she went, staring into the old lady's dark eyes. *What happened to you, Florence?* she wondered.

The old woman in the photograph blinked.

Sue stared in shock, in disbelief. The woman stared back, immovably frozen in time.

I must have imagined it, Sue thought.

But then the old woman in the photograph mouthed a single silent word: *Go.*

Sue let go of the frame. It hit the tiled hearth and the glass smashed.

Rick rushed back into the lounge room. "What was that? Are you all right?" He squatted down and picked up the frame, shaking loose shards of glass from it. "Did it slip off the mantelpiece?"

"The old lady spoke to me."

He stood up and put the picture back on the mantle, chuckling, but stopped when he saw the expression on her face.

"She told me to go."

Rick licked his lips. "It's a photo, babe."

Sue shook her head.

He took her by the hand. "Come on, let's check out the bedroom."

She followed him in a daze.

"Hey, look," Rick said. "A brass bed."

The bedhead was black wrought iron decorated with brass knobs and floral porcelain fittings, the pretty linen all frills and lace.

Rick put his arms around her and pulled her onto the bed with him. Of course, she was tired from the flight, she had just imagined that thing in the photograph. She relaxed into his embrace. He nuzzled his face into her neck, kissing her under her ear where she was ticklish. She squealed and bunched her shoulders. He kissed her ear and her cheek, and then his mouth met hers, his lips soft and warm. Her heart began to race. But when he slid his hand to her breast, she nimbly rolled aside and slid off the bed to her feet.

"Uh, uh…" She winked. "First things first, lover boy. Let's finish the tour. You promised me a wine cellar *par excellence*. First I need to powder my nose, and then," she raised her eyebrows, "then we'll see."

He grinned wolfishly. "To the cellar. After me, my love."

The entrance to the wine cellar was in the kitchen at the back of the house, beside an old-fashioned wood-fired Aga cooker. When Rick unlocked the door and pulled it open, there was a waft of cool, earthy air. Sue could see nothing beyond the first few steps; the wooden stairs descended into inky blackness.

Rick flicked a switch on the wall and a wan yellow light shone up to greet them. "Come on." He began to move down the stairs.

Sue grabbed his sleeve, overcome with sudden dread.

"What's wrong?"

She shook her head, unable to voice her emotions. Something did not feel right. Inexplicably, she felt terribly afraid.

"Still worried about spiders?" He laughed, took her hand and led her down into the cellar.

The single unshaded electric bulb illuminated the room with a muddy light. The cellar was surprisingly large, much bigger than Sue had expected. The furthest reaches that had been dug deep into the hill were shadowed and gloomy. The earthen floor was cool and the air felt slightly damp. Cobwebs were strung between the rows of chest-high racks loaded with wine bottles.

"Wow!" Rick said as he scurried from one rack to the next,

dusting a bottle here, squinting at a label there. He was like a child in a toyshop, barely looking at one thing before rushing to something else.

"Sue, look. *Grange*! You won't believe your eyes; it looks like the old boy laid down a case *every* year in the early days before it cost an arm and a leg."

Sue said nothing.

"Sue…?"

She was standing where he had left her, holding onto the bannister for support.

"What's wrong?"

"I don't know. I feel a bit woozy…" She gulped. "Maybe there's something wrong with the air down here."

Rick took a deep breath and exhaled. "Nope. Smells fine to me. Hey, you're trembling. Are you cold?"

Sue hugged herself. "Freezing. Take me out of here, Rick. I don't like it. I want to go back upstairs."

"Just let me grab a '55." He pulled out a bottle.

Sue turned towards the steps, but when she let go of the bannister her knees seemed to buckle beneath her. She had trouble drawing breath. She felt as though her lungs were full of mud. Then Rick was at her side, supporting her, leading her up the steps.

"What's the matter?"

She shuddered. "Just get me out of here."

They paused in the doorway while Sue took a few slow breaths, her anxiety draining away. Rick helped her to a seat at the kitchen table.

Sitting up naked in the brass bed with Rick, her thighs still damp from their lovemaking, Sue felt silly about her peculiar turn in the cellar.

The dizziness had left her almost as soon as they had returned to the kitchen. Indeed, she had felt fine. While Rick decanted the bottle of Grange she had opened their esky and prepared them marinated black olives, a simple cheese platter of ripe camembert, a sharp vintage cheddar, some aged gouda, and crackers. Then they had sat out on the front veranda and sampled the famous shiraz. They had talked and laughed, and before long they had taken the wine and glasses to the bedroom and made love.

Now, Rick poured them the last of the wine from the decanter, and sat back against his pillow with a contented sigh.

He raised his glass and breathed in the bouquet of the wine. "The nose on this '55 really is superb." He sipped the dark crimson liquid. "Amazing depth." He licked his lips. "Now I know why they say the '55 is one of the best wines ever made in Australia."

"Really?" Sue said teasingly. "I thought you always said there's no such thing as a great year, just great bottles?"

He laughed. "I know, but a *'55 Grange...* He poked his nose into the glass and inhaled. "Did you smell it? It's really wonderful."

Sue wafted the bed covers and the musky scent of their lovemaking surrounded them. She breathed deeply. "Mmm, yes, it smells wonderful." She grinned wickedly and snuggled up to him, her breasts pressing against his chest. "Let's do it again..."

Rick laughed, climbing out of bed. "Some recovery time might be in order. I'll get another bottle from the cellar first. To gird my loins, so to speak."

"I've had enough wine for the moment, Rick. Come back to bed. You're being a glutton."

"I'll just be a tick, babe." He picked up Great Uncle Enzo's fedora from the floor where he had tossed it earlier and slapped it jauntily on his head. "Wait right there. I'll get a bottle and open it so it can breathe for later."

Sue thought about what had happened to the poor old woman, Florence. Why she had never been found. What if she had been abducted?

A shiver ran down her back at the notion.

Sue looked at the time on her phone. Where was Rick? She pushed back the bed covers and crawled to the end of the bed. She listened hard for any sound of him, but the house was silent. Outside, trees swished in the breeze.

"Rick," she called. "What are you doing?"

But there was no reply.

She called again, a little annoyed now.

When he still did not answer, she got up, pulled the top sheet around her shoulders, and padded down the hall to find him.

She paused at the door to the lounge room. Rick wasn't there. To make sure, she went in and peered behind the sofa and *chaise longue*—just in case he was hiding, playing a silly game.

But the room was empty, just as they had left it.

Her gaze was drawn to the photograph of Florence and Enzo on the mantelpiece. She felt a strong compulsion to look at it again, to make eye contact with the old lady. She licked her lips and glanced furtively about. If Rick saw her he might think she was being silly. She went to the door and peered along the hallway. Still no sign of him. She crossed the room and took down the picture, careful not to cut herself on the shards of broken glass.

The couple stared back at her across the years.

"Do you really want us to leave?" she said softly.

Florence nodded.

Sue nearly dropped the frame again. Her heart began to race.

She stared at the picture but nothing else happened.

"Are you a ghost or a spirit?"

Florence nodded again, this time almost imperceptibly.

Was this really happening, Sue wondered? Now she wished Rick was with her so he could see this too, confirm she was not going crazy.

"What happened to you?"

Florence stared back and made no attempt to reply.

Maybe speaking was too difficult for her, Sue thought. It could be that she had used up all her energy, whatever and wherever she was, with that initial warning. Sue considered how to phrase her next question, realising that Florence could perhaps only nod or shake her head.

She took a deep breath. "Were you murdered?"

Another almost imperceptible nod, even smaller than the one before.

Sue realised she needed to get to the point. Florence was getting weaker. What should she ask? What was Florence trying to tell her?

Sue's mouth was dry and the words came out almost in a whisper. "Was it Enzo?"

Did Florence nod again? Sue stared hard at the photograph.

She steeled herself. "Are you trying to warn us about something?"

Nothing.

"Florence?"

Sue exhaled slowly. She shivered and pulled the sheet more closely around herself.

By the time she reached the kitchen, she began to feel distinctly uneasy.

Where was Rick?

Then she heard muffled sounds coming from the cellar.

She crossed the room and pulled open the door. The cellar light was on. Someone was singing. In *Italian*. It was punctuated every so often by a metallic scraping sound.

"Rick, is that you?" *I didn't know he could speak Italian*, she thought. "What are you doing?"

She ventured down the steps, careful not to trip on the trailing ends of the sheet still wrapped around her. At the foot of the stairs, she stopped and stared.

Naked, but still sporting Enzo's fedora, Rick was singing at the top of his voice as he dug a shallow trench in the earthen floor of the cellar beyond the wine racks. He was so intent on his task he hadn't noticed her arrival.

She marched over to him, let go of the sheet and grabbed the handle of the shovel. The sheet slid from her shoulders and dropped to the ground.

"Rick! What the hell are you doing?"

He stopped singing, yanked the shovel from her grasp, tossed it aside, and looked her up and down. An uncharacteristic leer twisted his face. She took a step back and folded her arms self-consciously across her breasts. He bent down to pick up a half-full bottle of wine from where it was propped against a mound of freshly dug dirt. He took a swig and wiped his mouth with the back of his hand.

"I'm busy, leave me alone," he slurred in an Italian accent.

"Rick, what are you playing at? Are you drunk?" She made a grab for the bottle.

"*Vaffanculo!*" he cursed, and snatched it away.

"What's wrong with you?" Her mind was racing. Tears welled in her eyes. "What's with this silly Italian business?"

"I said, *fuck off.*"

She licked her lips, her gaze darting around the cellar. He had never behaved like this before. She took another step back.

"Don't you dare speak to me like that."

He ogled her. Her lower lip began to tremble. He sneered and glanced from her to the hole he had dug.

He was like a different person. She studied him, trying to ascertain what it was, what had caused his change in behaviour.

"Why are you wearing that silly hat?"

"It's my favourite *cappello.*"

Realisation began to dawn on her. "Yes, of course it is," she said mildly. "I like it. Can I have a look at it?"

She stepped forward and reached out to remove it from his head.

Rick swung the bottle of wine at her like a bludgeon.

She ducked, but it caught her a glancing blow on the side of the head. For a split-second, she literally saw stars, then everything went black.

Sue came around gradually. She felt sick. Her head thumped with a blinding headache. Her face was pressed into cold, damp earth. She could smell—taste—its loamy substance.

Somewhere nearby, Rick was muttering to himself in Italian. *Italian.*

Oh, God, she thought. What was happening? What had happened to Rick? Was he possessed? Had he turned into some kind of psychopath? Had he lured her here into a trap? She couldn't believe he was a madman, but she struggled to accept the possibility that he had been taken over, even though she could find no other explanation.

Whatever the case, she was petrified, afraid to move in case he noticed her. If he saw she was awake he might strike her with the shovel, anything...

Then Rick started to sing again, a melancholy tune.

She turned her head slightly and realised she was lying face down in the shallow pit he had dug. She could feel the grit and stones pressing into her flesh.

She raised her head ever so slowly to see where he was.

Rick didn't notice her. He kept singing. He sat against the cellar wall, his knees drawn up, nursing a bottle of wine.

As she lowered her head, she noticed something glint in the earth beside her. Sue inched her hand to the spot and brushed at the dirt. She stifled a gasp. She had unearthed a skeletal hand. A gold wedding ring hung loosely on one of the yellowed, bony fingers.

She should have been scared, terrified. But instead, she felt attracted, oddly drawn to it. Sue took the skeletal hand into her own and images and knowledge flashed into her mind.

...Florence and Enzo arguing.

...Enzo drunk and violent. Time and again.

...Until the fateful night when Florence had tried to stop him drinking by blocking the door to the cellar and he had pushed her down the stairs.

...But the fall had not killed her. No. Enzo had buried his wife alive.

Once again, Sue could taste dirt. It seemed to fill her mouth, her nose, her lungs...

She couldn't breathe. She thought her chest would burst. Her vision turned red, went dark—

Then the smash of breaking glass broke the spell.

Sue let go of the skeletal hand and gasped. *Breathe*, she told herself. Glorious air filled her lungs, her vision returned. Understanding blossomed.

Enzo had returned to the scene of his crime. That's what Florence had been trying to tell her.

Sue didn't know what to do. She was trembling with cold and fear. But if she didn't act quickly, she expected she would permanently end up sharing the trench with Florence.

Slowly, she raised her head again to peer over the edge of the hole. Rick was standing unsteadily in front of one of the wine racks, pulling out one bottle after another, squinting at their labels. Then he cursed and tossed one aside. It smashed somewhere over near the stairs.

The sound made her flinch. The odour of earthy red wine filled the air.

She cast about for some way out. It was now or never. The shovel was on the ground where Rick had left it. She climbed to her knees, her head still throbbing, her heart in her throat, and scrambled out of the trench.

She stood for a moment considering the shovel. In her mind's eye, she snatched it up and bashed Rick on the head. A blow like that would stop him, possibly kill him. Was that what she wanted? A voice deep inside urged her to do it, incited her to put an end to him. But it didn't *feel* right, didn't feel like it was coming from her. This was the man she loved, the man she hoped to marry.

Instead, she launched herself at Rick. She hit him hard with her shoulder. He went down, and in that instant, she tore Enzo's hat off his head.

Sue sprang to her feet and backed away, sobbing with a mix of fear and anticipation, the fedora pressed tightly to her chest.

Rick lay still for a moment.

She crumpled the hat, tossed it into the trench, and grabbed the shovel. Holding it ready, she watched him, hardly daring to breathe.

"Sue...?" he croaked.

"Rick?" she said in a tremulous voice.

"Babe..." There was no trace of an Italian accent.

She dropped the shovel and helped him to his feet. He was unsteady, dazed and drunk, barely able to stand. She hugged him, holding him tight, his body cold against her own, then took his hand and dragged him staggering across the cellar towards the stairs.

He blinked in confusion and glanced back at the trench, but she jerked him forward.

Near the stairs, she yelped in pain and came to an abrupt halt. She had trodden on a piece of broken wine bottle. She could feel the shard in her foot, but she pressed on, leaving a trail of bloody prints.

They had to keep going. They had to get out.

She lurched up the stairs with Rick stumbling in tow. When they reached the kitchen, he collapsed to his knees. She banged the cellar door shut and slid to the floor beside him, breathing heavily. Her head was pounding. She touched it tentatively and flinched when she found a large painful lump beneath sticky, crusted hair. Her fingers came away stained with blood.

Rick reached an arm out towards the cellar, his hand opening and closing like that of an infant who can't quite reach a favourite toy.

Sue scrambled to her hands and knees, and heaved herself upright. She moved around behind Rick, took hold of him under his arms. She dragged him across the kitchen and managed to get him halfway down the hall before she stumbled and dropped him.

"Come on, Rick, help me," she pleaded, tears streaming down her cheeks.

He mumbled incoherently.

Her one thought was to get them both out of the house. Away from Enzo's and Florence's influence, beyond their reach.

Rick sat up and turned to look back the way they had come, towards the cellar.

"Snap out of it." She grabbed him by the shoulders and shook him.

He peered at her through glazed eyes.

"Get up, Rick." She took his hands in hers and tried to pull him up.

"Orright," he slurred as he half-clambered and was half-dragged back to his feet.

Panting, Sue led him by the hand to the front door. She undid the latch and pulled, but the door was stuck. She let go of Rick, grabbed the knob with both hands and yanked it hard. The door came open and cool night air blew on her flushed face.

"*Putana!*" Rick suddenly bellowed in Italian.

Sue spun around in alarm.

He had the walking stick from the hall stand — Enzo's walking stick — raised over his shoulder like a worker wielding a pickaxe.

"Rick, no! She lifted her arms to protect her face.

"Fucking *putana*." He brought the heavy stick down across her bare shoulder with a loud *thwack*.

She screamed in pain. Felt something snap. Her arm went limp, hanging uselessly at her side. But spurred on by a rush of adrenaline, she brought her knee up hard into Rick's groin.

He doubled over in agony. She grabbed a handful of his hair in her good hand and kneed him in the face.

The impact made a horrible crunch.

The walking stick clattered to the polished floor boards.

Dragging Rick by the hair, Sue lurched out the front door. She stumbled naked, broken and bleeding into the night, hauling Rick behind her.

The Wine Cellar — Afterword

There was a time in my life, when I worked in the corporate IT world, and I knew people just like Rick and Sue. Yuppies, some might call them. They were people who worked hard and played hard, and had plenty of disposable income. They lived a life of restaurants and fine wine; indeed, aside from sex, it was pretty much their existence outside of the long hours at the office.

I wondered what would happen if a couple of these IT people, who are typically highly intelligent and motivated, came face to face with ghostly entities haunting not a house *per se*, but objects left behind in the house…

'The Wine Cellar' is original to this collection.

Pest Control

"Fireball Lights up Night Sky"
Yahoo 7 News
Monday, December 10, 2012

A fiery green meteor lit up Melbourne's sky around 10:55 last night, triggering a rash of calls to emergency services and media outlets. Eyewitnesses report seeing a brilliant emerald fireball blaze across the night sky and explode in a starburst above the Dandenong Ranges east of the city. Fragments are said to have come down over the nearby hills.

Dr Joseph D'souza, Senior Curator of Geosciences at Museum Victoria, is keen to hear from anyone who witnessed a meteorite impact.

"It's quite rare for extraterrestrial fragments to fall to Earth," he said. "Only one in a thousand fireballs actually drops meteorites. If we can find and study these pieces of alien matter they might help us better understand the origins of our solar system, and perhaps even the universe."

The trouble started when the moths arrived.

They appeared about a week ago, fluttering out of the pantry in alarm when I opened the door. My house is on a bush block in the foothills of the Dandenongs so I'm used to sharing it with all sorts of bugs. It's not uncommon for me to see ants trooping across my kitchen wall, slaters in the bathroom, and spiders dangling from the ceiling on gossamer threads. So at first I didn't pay the moths much attention.

It wasn't until they started to flit across my line of sight when I was watching TV and flap around my bed lamp when I was reading at night, that I began to realise I had a problem. But even then I had no idea they heralded danger beyond my comprehension. It was the discovery of their pale maggot-like larvae partying in a packet of sugar that drove me to action.

I threw the sugar into the trash and went on a mini-rampage, swatting every moth that made the mistake of landing within my reach. I even managed to snatch a few of the critters out of the air as they fluttered about. They were small grey-brown things that virtually turned to dust in my clenched fist. But I knew my assault wasn't enough to get rid of them, so I googled the problem.

A seemingly authoritative website advised me to:

Throw away *all* packaged food.

Remove everything else from the cupboard and wash both the products and shelves thoroughly with a vinegar solution. Place environmentally friendly supermarket purchased moth traps on the shelves.

Simple.

So I tossed every single packet of flour, rice, cereal, pasta, sugar, biscuits, nuts and dried fruit into the garbage. There must have been two hundred dollars' worth of otherwise good food. Then I spent another two hours cleaning everything else and setting the traps.

It all seemed to go reasonably well, except that every so often I caught a whiff of something unpleasant. Particularly around the lower shelf. Like something turning rotten. But when I looked for the source of the odour the groceries smelled okay and the cupboard appeared blemish free.

I had trouble getting to sleep that night. I heard a rhythmic gnawing sound strike up shortly after I went to bed, and it put my nerves on edge. I tossed and turned for ages. I kept telling myself to relax, that there was nothing to worry about, but the feeling wouldn't go away, the sound wouldn't stop, and sleep continued to elude me.

Eventually, I got out of bed and headed downstairs to the kitchen to get a glass of milk. I could hear the peculiar gnawing noise all the way down, but it stopped suddenly when I switched on the kitchen light. I wondered if it might have been coming from outside, so I opened the front door and went out onto the porch. But the night was quiet and still.

I went back inside and forgot about the noise, because I could suddenly smell a putrid odour in the kitchen. My questing nose led me back to the pantry, but when I got down on my knees I couldn't see anything amiss. I would have to wash everything with a bleach solution in the morning, I decided, and made my way back upstairs to bed.

The rhythmic gnawing sound started again as soon as my head hit the pillow and I began to wonder if the noise was in my head, something to do with blood pressure, or perhaps some form of tinnitus. Whatever it was, it continued to keep me awake most of the night, relentlessly grinding and rasping.

When I got up in the morning, irritable and bleary-eyed, I made my way back down to the kitchen. Thankfully the odour seemed to have gone, so I switched on the kettle and went to check the pantry. When I opened the door I was astonished to find first one, then another, then another, all of the moth traps, choked with dead and dying moths. It was like nothing I'd ever seen—impossible. There simply could not have been that many moths in my whole house. But there they were in front of my eyes, covering the sticky inner surfaces of the traps in a thick, dusty grey-brown carpet.

I got down on my hands and knees to examine the bottom shelf and did a double take. There was a knot of tiny larvae in the corner, crawling and wriggling over each other in a pale, writhing mass; gnawing at the edges of a coin-sized hole in the right-hand back bottom corner of the shelf. But even as I watched in stunned fascination the caterpillars suddenly began to abandon their efforts and disappear into the hole, as if to escape my gaze.

I got down close, gagging as I caught a cloying whiff of something putrid, and tried to peer into the hole. I couldn't see anything, but I could hear something. Something familiar. It was the same gnawing sound that had kept me awake in the night, but now it was coming from the gap in the corner of my pantry. It sounded slightly different, like it was echoing in some vast empty space, but it was the *same* sound.

What's more, I got the bizarre impression there was something alive in the hole. More than an impression... I *knew* there was something there. Something much, much larger than a rat or possum that one might expect to find nesting in a wall cavity. Something vast. I could sense a pale, pulsing thing gnawing relentlessly in immense darkness beyond the tiny opening.

Then I felt the thing perceive *me*, felt it pause its ravenous gnawing and slowly turn to leer in my direction.

As its gaze found me, the room began to spin.

I clutched at the pantry door to steady myself, but it made no difference. It was worse than being paralytically drunk. Everything that should have been stationary and solid was suddenly gyroscoping around me in a dizzying blur of broken, swirling images.

My head was pounding.

The putrid smell from the cupboard rose up and hit me in the face like a piece of maggoty roadkill.

I fell to my knees, gagging on bitter bile.

Then the floor seemed to shift beneath me, as though a trapdoor had been released, and I was falling...

Falling end over end, somersaulting into a black void.

I found myself flying through space in a sort of lucid dream. The dizziness and nausea left me as suddenly as they had struck.

There was a shrill whistling in my ears, and I was soaring past planets, stars and primordial gas clouds toward the outer reaches of the cosmos.

There, in the otherwise emptiness of deep space, I came upon a cold uninviting planet, little more than a lump of bleak, grey stone bathed in a sickly, wan green light.

I fell into orbit around the planet and observed vast wintry deserts of black crystalline sands, I glided over churning oceans of thick dark ooze, and soared over forests of crawling grey fungus. Then I heard the familiar loathsome gnawing sound emanating from the very core of the desolate globe.

I knew straight away it was the pale, bloated worm-like thing gnawing at the core of this dead world. What's more, I could sense things *about* the world-gnawing creature. Uncomfortable alien things I did not want to know. I became aware of its callous disdain, and of its terrible ravenous hunger. Worst of all, it was a two-way street, and it now knew about *me*, and through me about our world, our universe.

I was the conduit, the roadmap, the opener of the way!

And it was coming…

A pantry moth flew into my face and the connection broke.

I pulled back with a jerk and crouched, stunned, on the kitchen floor. I looked back into the pantry, but all I could see were a few horrible little larvae still nibbling at the edge of the hole, miniature parodies of the world-gnawing thing I had…

What?

Daydreamed?

Fantasised?

But I had *seen* it, *felt* it, and it had seen me.

Was I going crazy? Could that rank odour be some sort of gas, have some sort of hallucinogenic effect? Did I have a tumour pressing on my brain? My rational mind told me the monstrous alien creature could not be real, that there must be some explanation, but my gut reaction was to flee because I could still feel its hideous hunger, its burning desire to cross over into our world.

It was coming…

And it made me feel insignificant and vulnerable.

After some deep breathing, a cup of strong, sweet tea, and a good dose of self-therapy, I managed to bring my mind back to the here and now, to the practical problem at hand. I decided the best thing to do was to stick to my original strategy and get rid of the moths and caterpillars. They still seemed to be the link between our world and the creature gnawing at the heart of the cold, dark planet of my vision.

I went down to the local shops and came home with a bag full of insect spray and naphthalene moth repellent. First I emptied an entire can of surface insect spray into the bottom shelf of the pantry, taking care to soak the area around the hole in the back corner of the cupboard. Then I followed that with another entire can of flying insect killer for good measure.

The fumes from the insect sprays were so strong my eyes stung and I began to feel light headed, but I wasn't ready to stop. I finished the job by pouring two large packets of naphthalene onto the pantry shelf, piling the pungent flakes into a heap so they completely covered the hole in the corner.

Take that, you little pests, I thought.

But later that day when I went to check my handiwork, I found the kitchen inundated with a cloying stench that made me feel sick. Not the eye-watering smell of insect spray and naphthalene, but the horrible rotting putrescence that was the mark of the worm.

I rushed to the pantry cupboard and flung open the doors. Inside, the naphthalene flakes had all but gone! The few crumbs that were left were being devoured by pale, wriggling caterpillars that squirmed back into the hole when the kitchen light poured in.

I had doused them with poison and covered them with repellent, but instead of killing them I had simply fed the little buggers.

Even worse, the hole itself was bigger, the size of a tennis ball, as if the naphthalene had energised the larvae, increasing their strength and appetite as though they'd been fed steroids. It didn't make sense. With the amount of chemicals I'd poured in I should have killed every flying, crawling, and wriggling creature within cooee.

I got back down on my hands and knees to try to see into the hole. I dared whatever I had previously seen—or imagined I had seen—to move again, to prove that it was there, that it was real. But the harder I looked, the more I saw nothing. Just a deep inky blackness.

Then the blackness shifted. The curvature changed or the light refracted differently, and I realised I was staring not into space, but into an enormous eye! An alien eye that was pressed against the other side of the hole to better see into our world.

Looking into my kitchen, watching me…

I lunged for the utensil drawer, and grabbed the first implement that came to hand. I had hoped for a bread knife or metal skewer, but instead I came up with a wooden spoon. It would have to do, I decided, and thrust it handle-first into the hole, into the watching eye.

There was a brief moment of resistance, then it gave way and the offending eyeball burst with a squidgy pop.

The creature screamed. The wooden spoon was jerked out of my hand.

Thick yellow slime splashed onto my hand and I yelped.

It burned. It was like acid, like scalding steam.

I jumped up, swearing, and leaped to the kitchen sink where I thrust my hand under the cold tap. The water washed the remaining slime off and soothed the pain temporarily, but when I took my hand out from the water it burned anew.

What the hell was it?

I had no idea, but I knew one thing: it was not the enormous worm-like thing I had seen gnawing at the core of the far-flung dead world. It was far too small. Miniscule in comparison, so

perhaps it was some sort of spawn? Maybe one of its parasites?
Who knew?

But whatever it was, it foreshadowed the coming of the Eater of Worlds, proved the way was opening.

After that I stopped trying to explain what was happening with everyday logic. I knew the hideous truth for what it was, knew that the hole in the pantry somehow led to another universe, or another dimension, or whatever. A cold, dark place inhabited by a fetid behemoth and its spawn, parasites and vermin. Worst of all, I knew that the gargantuan, world-gnawing worm had invited itself for dinner, and it planned to arrive on planet Earth through my kitchen cupboard.

Funnily enough, with this realisation came the knowledge that I held the fate not only of mankind, but the very fabric of our universe in my hands. *Me*, of all people. I guess I could have called for help, but who would have believed me? "Hello, police? There's an alien monster trying to come through a hole in my kitchen cupboard." They would've locked me up, probably in a straight jacket.

Shit, I hardly believe what's happening myself.

Which is why I'm furiously typing this blog entry on my laptop while I sit waiting on a kitchen chair in front of the pantry. Thank God for wireless internet. It means I can get the message out while I wait for my nose to detect the stench of putrid decay, or for my ears to hear the appalling gnawing sound, heralding the opening of the gate.

I have a jerry can full of petrol, a box of kerosene-impregnated firelighters, toxic sprays of various formulas, and an assortment of tools and kitchen implements including a sledge hammer and meat cleaver. Even the old .22 rifle I keep hidden in the rafters. I just hope it's enough. Wish me luck, dear reader, for if I fail not only will the blasphemous world-gnawing worm come through, but I suspect a whole other universe or dimension will spill through with it.

"Man Believed Dead in Fire"
Leader Free Press
Wednesday, December 19, 2012

Police believe that Belgrave man, Mr Jonathan Shapiro, perished when his hillside house mysteriously burned to the ground during the early hours of Monday morning. Captain Richard Weeks from the Country Fire Authority said the fire was so intense that by the time CFA crews arrived, it was all they could do to stop the blaze spreading to neighbouring houses. Firemen on the scene reported smelling fumes and noticed an unusual green tinge to the flames. Police are treating the fire as suspicious and have asked anyone with information to call Crime Stoppers.

Pest Control — Afterword

In this story, I set out to leverage a common pulp fiction technique. H. P. Lovecraft and others of his contemporaries who wrote stories in the golden era of *Weird Tales* often had lone narrators facing unspeakable horrors. But I wanted to raise the form above its somewhat hackneyed pulp history by placing it in a contemporary setting and applying modern sensibilities.

Using only a single character in a story makes it difficult to develop conflict, but I think I achieved a good balance between the old and the new. I lived in the house in which the events take place, and even had to deal with pantry moths.

I just hope I managed to seal up the dark hole in the back, right-hand corner of the cupboard…

'Pest Control' was first published in 2014 in *Cthulhu: Deep Down Under.*

Old Wood

Colin Travers went out early one Saturday morning in search of old wood. Heavy beams, preferably weathered and chunky. Timber with a bit of character.

His wife, Desley, was surprised when she heard his car pull up in the driveway only two hours later. Colin had told her he thought the search might take all day, perhaps even the following Saturday as well.

"Hey, Des," he called excitedly when he came in. "Check out what I found." He proffered a piece of wood that appeared decidedly old—mouldering, Desley thought.

"A lump of firewood," she said teasingly.

"Des, come on. This is just what I want for the pergola out the back. It's unbelievable. I got the whole lot for thirty bucks. And you'll never guess, but the old codger at the demolition yard where I bought it says it's antique; reckons it came over on the First Fleet." He ran the tips of his fingers along its weathered surface. "Hand hewn, I think." Colin squinted at it. "You can still see the tool marks if you look closely." He thrust it at Desley. "Have a feel."

"Come on, Colin." Desley pushed it distastefully aside. "Don't tell me you believe that stuff. It's probably just an ordinary piece of grotty old wood. What I'm concerned about is whether or not it'll look any good."

Colin shrugged. "Maybe the old boy did spin me a yarn. Either way, it was cheap and this pergola will look just great."

He stroked the piece of wood with obvious regard. "I'm going to get started on it straight away."

Later that evening, Desley watched Colin through the kitchen window while she absentmindedly washed the dinner dishes. Despite the fact that it was cold and nearly dark outside, Colin was still working on the pergola.

From the very moment he started work he had attacked the job as if driven, stopping only grudgingly to eat. Now, by the yellowish glow of the outside light, he grunted and heaved, positioning the second of the heavy vertical support posts in place.

Desley slid the window over the sink open. "Come on, Colin, it's late. Why don't you call it a day?"

"Soon," he snapped. Then more genially he added, "I've got to brace this upright in place until the concrete sets." But Colin pottered around for some time after he fixed the braces in place. By the time Desley had finished the evening's chores and changed in front of the heater for bed, he still hadn't come in.

She was in two minds about Colin's sudden enthusiasm to get the job done. She admired his commitment, but couldn't help feeling doubtful about the finished product. She had wanted the pergola built from treated pine, but Colin had set his mind on something old and rustic.

Turning back the bedcovers, Desley heard the pitter-patter of raindrops hitting the roof. She sat on the bed, listening, waiting for Colin to come in, and then got angry when he didn't. Finally she went to call him, as though he were a child having to be reminded not to stay out in the rain.

She flung the back door wide and saw him standing motionless in the chilling downpour, staring up at one of the upright posts as though in a trance. She called his name and, just as he was indifferent to the rain drops striking his face, he seemed not to hear her.

With no other choice, Desley splashed across the rain-puddled veranda and grabbed him by the arm.

"Colin!"

He gasped. "Huh?" He blinked at her, disoriented.

"Come inside you bloody idiot. You're soaked."

"Oh…" He looked down at his sodden clothes in confused disbelief. "…yeah."

When they made love that night Colin went through the physical motions, but his mind wandered elsewhere. Long after Desley had gone to sleep he lay awake in the dark trying to collect his thoughts. There were mutterings, elusive voices lurking in some recess of his mind. The voices were accompanied by fleeting visions, indistinct, but visible to his mind's eye like movements seen from the corner of one's own eye. Yet try as he might he could not focus on these disquieting shadows.

Eventually he succumbed to his tiredness and drifted into a deep sleep, untroubled and dreamless until the early hours of the morning when he began to moan softly, writhing between the sheets. He cried out and began to wail and thrash his arms and legs wildly.

Desley sat up, startled, frightened. She flicked on the bedside lamp and stared at Colin. His face was contorted into a grotesque mask and her immediate thought was he was in the throes of some sort of seizure.

Then it dawned on her that he was still asleep, caught in the clutches of some violently uncharacteristic nightmare. But the moment she reached over and touched him he fell quiet and limp, as though her fingertips had administered some powerful sedative. His face was relaxed, the rhythm of his breathing easy as he slept peacefully once more.

It was then Desley noticed the trace of an odour. For some reason it made her feel curiously uncomfortable. It was an unusual yet vaguely familiar smell, dry and dusty, like old hessian sacks. But try as she might she could not recognise it or place its source. At one stage it seemed to be emanating from Colin himself. Then the odour was gone. She sniffed here and there, but the only scents to meet her searching nostrils were familiar and comforting.

For a time she lay awake, wondering what had disturbed Colin, listening to the regular sound of his breathing. Eventually she fell asleep, still puzzled she was unable to identify the dusty odour.

In the morning when Desley awoke, Colin had already risen. She found him standing in the kitchen staring out the window at the two tall posts he had erected the day before. As she watched he began to rock his head from side to side while he massaged the back of his neck.

"Morning," she said. "Want some breakfast?"

Colin started to turn towards her, then froze mid-motion with a grunt. He grimaced. "Yeah."

"What's wrong?"

"I dunno, I must've slept funny or something. I've got a stiff neck this morning."

"You probably pulled a muscle thrashing about in that terrible nightmare last night. You were yelling out and everything. I was really worried. I nearly woke you up but you went quiet."

He was rubbing the back of his neck again, only half listening, his attention on the structure outside. "Yeah? I don't remember a damn thing. Anyway, how long's breakfast going to be? I've got to get back to work."

Ten minutes later, after gulping down toast and coffee, Colin set to on the pergola with similar gusto to that of the previous day. He drilled holes near each end of the horizontal cross beam, making sure the bolts that would soon hold it up passed freely through.

Then, with a lot of heaving and grunting and the aid of an

old tow rope he'd found in the garage, Colin hauled the beam up until it was positioned precariously in place ready for fixing.

He would have worked right through lunch but Desley brought out two thick ham and salad sandwiches and a can of beer just as he finished bolting the long cross beam into place. She insisted he stop and eat, then stared in amazement as he wolfed down the meal like a man who has not seen food for a week.

"You really needed that," she said. "Do you want some more?"

Colin slowly stood up. He pulled the ring tab on his can of beer, threw back his head, and swilled the whole can down his throat making his Adam's apple bob wildly. Then he burped loudly and sighed, wiping his chin with his sleeve before he replied.

"Just bring me more ale," he blurted, beer spraying in her face, "then leave me to get on with it."

Desley's bottom lip trembled. "Get it yourself you ungrateful pig!" She dashed the empty beer can from his grasp and ran inside the house.

When she had gone Colin returned to work as though nothing had happened. He cut and drilled two smaller pieces of timber so he could brace the structure diagonally in each corner. Finally, when the braces were in place, he tightened the bolts with a pair of shifting spanners until the washers began to make impressions in the wood.

It was solid. Colin walked around the frame admiring his handiwork. He shook one of the vertical posts and there was surprisingly little movement. To anyone watching, his pride was obvious.

Desley looked out in annoyance from the kitchen and thought the frame looked like an oversized soccer goal. As she watched, Colin continued to pace around it, stopping to view it from different angles. He seemed entranced, mesmerised by the thing. Gone now was his gusto to continue building. In fact, he did no more work for the rest of the day.

Sometime after midnight Desley awoke feeling strangely on edge, as if half-expecting impending danger. She had the impression a noise had disturbed her and she listened intently; Colin's breathing was easy and regular. Far away a car door slammed, an engine roared into life, faded into the distance. Then the wind picked up and she heard it. An irregular slapping sound somewhere out the back.

She rose quietly and made her way to the kitchen where the sound was louder. When she switched on the outside light she could see it was the rope Colin had left dangling from the pergola frame. It was dancing in the breeze, slapping noisily against the beams. Cursing under her breath, she returned to bed.

In the darkness, she lay thinking about Colin's uncharacteristic moodiness, his irritation and impatience with her; it wasn't her imagination, he seemed to be changing. In the space of two days he had become a virtual stranger.

The sound of Colin's voice interrupted Desley's thoughts. He was talking in his sleep again, except this time his voice was not his own... It was a stranger's voice, frightening, rasping, thick with brogue. A voice Desley had never heard Colin use before. She listened intently but much of what he said was mumbled or inaudible. She could only pick up snatches of it: "I didn't do it... Oh, the pain...the ecstasy...show him how it feels..."

His voice trailed off into an unintelligible growl, unexpectedly changing pitch, alerting Desley something was wrong. Then once again she smelled the unusual odour she had encountered the previous night. Inexplicably, terror struck her. She threw off the bed covers and hit the light switch. Colin's legs began to twitch spasmodically and his mouth was hanging wide open as he continued to make the strange sound.

She grabbed his shoulders and shook him violently but it had no effect. "Colin! Colin!" Still he would not wake. Now the sound he made was like bath water going down a plughole. His nostrils were flared and his thickening lips had taken on a bluish appearance.

Desley struck his face with all the force she could muster. Once. Twice. "Colin!" she screamed, and hit him again.

Suddenly his eyelids flew open and he lurched forward gasping for breath. Great chest-heaving, painful gasps that racked his entire body. Gasps that brought a healthy red colour back to his face and quenched the painful burning in his lungs. Slowly his breathing eased and he fell back exhausted.

"Are you all right?" Desley asked, her fingers digging into his arm.

He nodded between gulps. "I'm okay—it was just a dream."

"Just a dream! You were choking. I thought you were dying." Tears welled up and glazed her eyes.

"I'll be fine." He rubbed his neck. "I just need a drink of water."

"Oh Colin, I think you should see a doctor. Look at the bed, you've wet the bed."

"I said I'll be fine," he snapped, rising from the bed. "Just change the bloody sheets."

As she replaced the soiled bed linen, Desley heard him at the kitchen sink: the clink of glass, the sound of running water. Then for a long time there was silence. She imagined him staring out the window into the darkness at that structure.

Finally, when he returned Colin rolled over with his back to Desley and went to sleep. She lay awake for a long time both cursing and worrying about him, once again trying to place that unsettling, vaguely familiar smell.

The next morning was Monday: back to work for both Colin and Desley. As usual, Desley rose about half an hour after Colin because he had to leave first. She felt exhausted, having been awake half the night worrying about him and his strange dreams, and for the first few minutes she moved about the house in a bleary-eyed daze.

Desley first realised something was wrong when she found the kettle was cold. Next she discovered Colin was not in the bathroom and had not taken his morning shower. Somehow the house felt abnormally still; she couldn't hear him anywhere.

Then she noticed the back door was ajar.

She found him shuffling around outside clad only in his pyjamas. Barefooted, he was stooped and bedraggled, his head low, his hands clasped behind his back. "Colin!" She ran to him, grasping his arm.

He looked at her, eyes blinking, confused, dazed. And she saw his neck.

"Oh my God! Colin what's happened to you? What are you doing out here?"

"I…ah, I don't feel too good…"

"Your neck, it's all red and bruised! Colin, what's going on? First you act like a stranger, then those weird dreams—my God, I thought you were going to choke last night—now this."

"I'll be all right, just leave me alone."

"You're not all right! You've got to see someone. I'll stay home and take you to see the doctor." Desley grasped his shoulders, turned him to face the house and walked him towards it.

"No!" He stopped. "I mean, I'm not a child. There's no need for you to miss work. I can go by myself."

"Then promise you'll go this morning?"

"Yeah, now leave me alone will you? Get off my back."

"No, not until you come inside. I don't know what you think you're doing, but you'll catch bloody pneumonia out here dressed like that."

Colin mumbled something about fresh air and then fell silent as Desley led him in by the arm.

On the drive to work a short while later Desley felt a headache coming on and wished she'd stayed home. She already felt sick in the stomach worrying about Colin; in his present state she had real doubts about the glib assurances he had given.

Then there was that peculiar smell that continued to haunt her, like jute or hemp…or rope. And that made her think of the flapping rope that had awakened her the previous night.

On top of everything else, this feeling—the importance of the smell—seemed to take on greater proportions. The hammer continued to pound in her skull and her stomach began to knot with creeping fear. It was too much. At the next set of traffic lights she made a tyre-screeching U-turn for home.

Desley now showed little care for the hazards of the road; she ran a red light but didn't even notice. She skidded the car to a halt in the driveway and fumbled at the front door with the keys.

Inside, she rushed from room to room calling Colin's name until she reached the kitchen. There she came to a halt when she saw the back door was open and fearfully turned to look out the window. She let out a sigh of relief when she saw Colin outside, but it quickly changed into a gasp when she realised what he was doing.

Desley plunged through the door with renewed frenzy, shrieking his name as she went. But Colin seemed oblivious to her; still barefoot and dressed in his pyjamas he was engrossed instead on knotting a hangman's noose at the end of the rope dangling from the pergola frame.

She grabbed Colin by the arm and tried to pull him away, but he growled menacingly. Desley yanked harder and he turned on her, shoving her away with such force she fell and twisted her ankle. Rising painfully, she broke into sobs, pleading with him. He growled again, baring his teeth like some wild beast.

"Colin, it must be something to do with the wood! That damned old wood," she cried. "Listen to me!"

Again she tried to wrench him away from his macabre handiwork. This time he struck her. Red and white sparks exploded behind her eyes. Even though it was only a glancing blow she was stunned. She dropped to her hands and knees.

Colin examined the finished noose and held it open so his head would fit through.

Desley cast her eyes desperately to and fro in search of assistance, anything, and her tear-blurred gaze came to rest on the remaining timber Colin had left scattered on the veranda. She crawled towards it and grasped a metre-long piece which she used as a crutch to pull herself to her feet. When she had her balance, she hefted it above her head like a club and lunged at Colin. The beam came down across the back of his neck with a thud. The impact jarred the wood from her grasp and it clattered to her feet.

Colin seemed to pause, swaying slightly, caught in the very act of placing the sinister noose over his head, before he crumpled, collapsing in an unconscious heap.

The jilted rope swung to and fro in the air above him.

Weeping fearfully, tears streaming down her face, Desley took hold of Colin's ankles and dragged him laboriously away from the makeshift gallows towards the house. Once she slipped and fell, her injured ankle shooting excruciating shards of pain up her leg, but she struggled to her feet and went painfully on. When finally she reached the back door, Desley dropped Colin's feet with a mighty sigh and fell on top of him, whimpering, hugging and kissing him, her tears spilling on his face.

She left him slumped by the doorway and limped about the yard collecting all the unused lumps of old wood, wildly hurling them into untidy piles around the two upright posts. Sobbing in fear and pain, she rushed into the garage for a can of mower fuel and splashed it liberally over the mounds of wood, pausing to pour some down each of the vertical beams. When the can was empty she tossed it aside and hobbled around Colin's prone form, into the house.

Moments later Desley re-emerged fumbling with a box of matches. Even from the doorway the smell of petrol from the pyres was pungent. She stepped hurriedly around Colin as he began to stir and groan but she wasn't quick enough. He lunged at her, and caught hold of her injured foot. Desley screamed, first in terror and then in agony as she kicked her foot free. But the effort threw her off balance and she lurched forward and hit the ground face first.

Matches sprayed from the box with the impact. Desley lay stunned for a moment but even before her senses had fully returned she was scrabbling for the loose matchsticks. She found one and struck it but the head failed to ignite. She struck it again. This time it broke as it flared into life and the burning

146

phosphorous head scorched the back of her hand. Sobbing, she groped for another match as she cast a furtive glance over her shoulder.

What she saw made her feel as though something heinous had taken hold of her heart and squeezed it; Colin looked like some enraged wild beast rising to his hands and knees, his teeth bared, his eyes burning with malicious intent. Desperately she groped for another match, struck it and threw it into the primed timber.

Nothing happened...

But as she began to fumble for another match the fuel ignited. There was a sudden flash, an explosive thump, and a blast of hot air washed over her. The post crackled as flames licked high into the air. Desley's eyes stung and she could smell the acrid odour of singed hair.

With still-trembling fingers, Desley groped again for the matches, but her search was halted when her arm was suddenly pinned, as though the jaws of a mighty hound had snapped shut on her forearm. She was twisted painfully around until she was face to face with Colin. His snarling face was hideous.

Desley struck at him, but he raised his arm and easily blocked her punch. She managed to duck under his retaliatory blow and tackled him around the belly, sending them both sprawling on the veranda.

They struggled, thrashing and clawing; Colin trying to get to the searing flames, Desley trying frantically to obstruct him.

Then, despite Colin's intervention, a second explosion rocked them and halted their struggle. A trail of petrol drips between the two posts had ignited the other pyre.

Roaring with anger and frustration, Colin surged to his feet with a herculean effort. He dragged Desley up with him. They began to rain blows on each other.

It was the screaming that stopped them. At first they didn't notice it, but it quickly built to such an unholy crescendo, that they fell apart and dropped to their knees, clasping their palms over their ears.

From the flames came a multitude of screams and wails so

intense they drilled their way into Desley's consciousness and seemed to explode.

She started to scream herself but fell silent, stricken when she saw the faces. One by one they were appearing in the fire; men and women scrambling frantically trying to escape the flames, imploring, abusing Desley. Their vile curses rising to profane wails.

A flaming beam collapsed, then began to rise as grotesque arms hauled it up. It began to take on a fiery human shape; its legs staggered wildly as it tried to balance, its arms flailed like a wild man. A bestial face, bearded by glowing fire, roared at them and lunged forward.

Desley tried to scream, but felt as though an icy hand was squeezing her throat. Her mouth worked soundlessly as the unuttered scream echoed in her mind. Finally, stricken with terror, the last remnants of strength deserted her and she crumpled to the ground before the blazing monstrosity.

The thing teetered, sensing her helplessness too late as the flames consumed it. Carried by its own momentum the fiery creature gave a hideous roar and collapsed onto the lawn in a shower of sparks, burning, disintegrating into crumbling ashes.

The blaze intensified for a few moments, as though revitalised by fuel, then gradually the faces began to vanish, burning up, their pain-filled expressions tortured, hideous, their mouths wailing in torment. The terrible din faded until finally it disappeared with the last of the grisly faces. The only remaining sound was the crackle of old wood burning. The smell of boiling blood—acrid and sweet—hung in the air.

Colin moaned and rose unsteadily to his feet, tenderly rubbing the back of his neck.

Cradling her injured ankle, Desley rolled over to face him. "Colin…are…are you all right now?"

"Yeah…I think so." He saw blood trickling from her nose, her eyes teary and blackened. He bent and helped her to her feet, staring slack-jawed at the fires, shocked, disoriented. "Des, my God! What's happening?"

Desley threw her arms around Colin and kissed him, tears of

joy and relief rolling down her cheeks. "Help me inside and I'll tell you, you bastard. And next time maybe you'll listen to me when I say I want treated pine."

Old Wood — Afterword

Back in the early nineties, a friend of mine employed a shipwright to build a pergola at the rear of his house. The shipwright fashioned the structure from ancient timber beams he had salvaged from who knows where. It was a work of rustic art, like nothing I had ever seen. The imagery of the pergola stayed with me, long after the house had changed hands, and the structure reappeared unbidden when I started to think about haunted objects.

Around the same time, I was undertaking some DIY renovations on my own home, like so many other young couples and families. It was interesting to observe the impact of renovating on people's relationships and lives.

Back then, I was what is known as a "discovery writer" rather than a "planner". I usually started with a character or a situation, maybe some idea of how it would end, and I would start writing to see what happened. As a result of this technique, I often had false starts and ended up with stories that went nowhere. But with 'Old Wood', all these individual ideas came together as a whole and resulted not only in a finished story, but one that has been quite popular.

It was originally published in *Terror Australis* magazine before being reprinted in the Penguin anthology *Strange Fruit*, edited by Paul Collins. In Kerry Greenwood's review of that book in *Meanjin*, she described the story as one of the best in the anthology.

The Sorcerer's Looking Glass

Three cloaked and hooded riders reined their steaming mounts to a halt and looked down into the misty valley below. It was dusk and the light was fading rapidly. The horses shuffled and snorted, puffing clouds of breath into the cool evening air.

"Castle Ammar, boys," announced the tallest of the three riders. He pointed to the dark stone stronghold, which looked like an island of parapets and turrets floating in a sea of mist. "Our new home."

"But, father, what of Khasis?" asked the boy named Yazir.

The man snorted. "The great sorcerer?" He chuckled softly. "You don't need to worry about Khasis, son. My troops have scoured every nook and cranny of the castle, even the secret rooms and tunnels, and there is no sign of him. I expect he's gone for good."

"Can we be sure, father?" the other boy asked. "Nobody saw him leave, nobody heard him go. For all we know he could have turned himself into a gargoyle and might even now be watching us from the rooftop."

The man smiled and shook his head kindly. "Ah, Mikal, what will I do with you?" He reached over and clapped the lad on his shoulder. "Put those thoughts out of your head. Would I bring you here if all was not well? The old villain probably disguised himself as a peasant and skulked away when my troops laid siege to the castle walls."

The boys' father spurred his horse forward. "Come on, let's not dally, Castle Ammar and a hot meal is waiting for us."

Stable lads hurried to meet the riders as they clattered across the castle drawbridge into the cobbled courtyard. Servants greeted them at the door. Yazir and Mikal were shown their new bedrooms, then they went to the kitchen where they warmed themselves by the stove. The brothers were ravenous after their long journey, and before long they were wolfing down steaming hotcakes drizzled with honey. The boys were tired, too, and really should have gone to bed. But they were unable to resist the temptation to explore the castle.

"Let's see if we can find the secret passages," said Yazir.

Then it was a race, first Yazir, then Mikal, running along silent stone corridors lit by lamplight, leaping down flights of stairs and careering around corners. When eventually they slowed, the boys found themselves in a small damp-smelling chamber, deep below the towering castle. A single guttering oil lamp cast a muddy yellow light.

"C'mon," Mikal said between breaths, as he turned to head back the way they had come. "Let's go." Something about this place made him uncomfortable.

"Yazir?"

There was no reply.

Mikal turned back. The chamber was empty. Across from him, a narrow corridor led away into darkness.

"Yazir!" he yelled.

There was a pause, followed by a muffled reply.

"Mikal! Here, quick."

Mikal followed Yazir's voice into the gloomy tunnel, carefully feeling his way along the rough-cut stone walls. Soon Mikal was in complete darkness. Even when he looked back there was no light, and he guessed the corridor must curve away from the entrance. Then he saw a halo of silvery light silhouetting his brother up ahead in the tunnel.

"Hurry up," urged Yazir.

"What?"

"Help me with this door," Yazir said. "This must be one of the secret rooms."

The heavy stone door was slightly ajar and Yazir was using

his shoulder and weight to try to force it open. Mikal joined him and together they both shoved.

Suddenly, the door gave way and scraped open.

Light spilled into the corridor and the boys stumbled excitedly into a room. But their elation was short-lived. Broken glass crunched under the soles of their boots. Clearly their father's soldiers had been here first. Whatever the room had once housed now lay smashed and broken in a jumbled heap of splintered wood, torn fabric, and broken pottery.

Silvery light spilled from a skylight and illuminated the room. "Moonlight," Yazir muttered. The floor and walls were smooth black granite, inlaid with white marble to form strange geometric symbols and star signs.

"This must have been Khasis' secret alchemy room," Mikal said.

But Yazir did not answer, his attention distracted by something else. He walked across to one of the walls where the figure of an eye seemed to be shining more vividly than the other symbols.

"Look at this."

A beam of moonlight, brighter than that coming through the skylight, shone through a hole high in the corner of the room, projecting a bright rectangle onto the wall.

"It looks like a door," Yazir said. He ran his fingers across the surface of the stone. "Mikal! There is a door here. I can feel the edge."

Mikal hurried to join him and together they pushed and shoved, but the stone would not budge.

"Try the symbol," Mikal said.

Yazir brushed his fingers across the black pupil of the eye, and something behind the wall fell with a heavy thud. Then with the grinding sound of stone grating on stone, part of the wall slid away to reveal an opening into which poured the beam of bright moonlight.

The brothers stood dumbfounded, staring at each other.

"I think we should get father," Mikal eventually said.

With the spell broken, Yazir moved. "Let's see what's in here first," he said, and stepped through the opening.

The room inside was tiny, empty except for a single piece of furniture. A tall mirror in a decoratively carved wooden frame, fixed between two upright posts so it could be tilted to adjust the viewing angle. Yazir adjusted it so he could see his reflection.

"A looking glass," Yazir said with delight. "It's mine. I found it."

"You can have it." Mikal looked from side to side over his shoulder. "I don't like this place. The glass is probably locked in here because it's enchanted."

"Don't be ridiculous, little brother." Yazir sniggered. "Don't you know silver glass has to be brought all the way from the Far East? It was probably hidden in here for safekeeping. One of Khasis's treasures. A looking glass as large as this is very rare. Lend me a hand, help me carry it outside."

Back in the room with the symbols, the boys could see the carved timber was a rich red-brown, waxed and polished to a high sheen. But the quality of the mirror glass itself was poor. Their reflections were distorted and unclear.

"It's just what I need for dressing," Yazir said. "It will go well in my bedroom." He took hold of the top of the mirror frame and tilted it back. "Come on, grab the other end."

"Hey!" Mikal clutched his brother by the arm. "What's that?"

"What?"

"There, in the looking glass. I saw something move."

Yazir pulled his arm free and gave his brother a scornful look. "What are you talking about?"

Mikal's face was pale, his dark eyes wide. He stared into the mirror, biting his bottom lip. "I saw a mist, or a fog, and there was a dark shape moving in it." His voice was almost a whisper.

Yazir tipped the mirror back onto its feet and peered into the glass. All he could see was his own distorted image.

"You're seeing things, Mikal." He punched his brother lightly on the arm. "I think you saw your own reflection."

Mikal slowly shook his head, still peering into the mottled glass. "Then how do you explain the mist? I saw a mist."

Yazir shrugged. "Dust or dirt? A reflection of the wall or ceiling when I tilted the looking glass?"

"I don't like it," Mikal said. He shivered and gave the mirror a suspicious appraisal. "I don't like it at all."

"Yazir..."

It came from faraway, soft but insistent. Yazir stirred in his sleep and rolled over. A girl's voice, alluring, beckoning, calling his name.

"Yazir..." Slightly louder.

He yawned and propped himself up on an elbow. Faint early-morning light squeezed through the gaps in the window shutters and fell across his bed. Birds were twittering and close by a rooster crowed. Sunrise. Who would be calling him at this time of morning? Whoever it was would wake up the whole castle if they kept it up.

"Yazir..." It was a pretty voice. Who could it be? A serving girl? Who else knew his name?

"Yazir." A pause. "Yazir..."

Definitely a girl's voice. Almost pleading. Yazir listened hard, waiting for the voice to come again so he could pinpoint its location.

"Yazir, help me..."

He sat up and looked around. The voice sounded as though it was coming from inside his room. His gaze fell on the sorcerer's looking glass, which stood in the corner.

"Yazir, help me. I'm trapped!"

If he didn't know better, Yazir could have sworn the voice had come from the mirror. He climbed out of bed and stood in front of the glass. At first his own fuzzy reflection stared back at him, but as he watched a faint mist began to swirl and obscure his image. A fog, just like Mikal said he'd seen last night.

Then Yazir saw the shadow. Something moved in the mist. He squinted, trying to make it out. Was it his imagination? His own reflection? No, it was moving and he was standing still. He peered harder but the mist began to thin and the image seemed to fade before his eyes.

"Ya-z-ir…" It trailed off as the last wisps of vapour disappeared and his distorted reflection stared back at him in astonishment.

Yazir crept into Mikal's room and quietly closed the door behind him. His younger brother was sound asleep, a small string of dribble hanging from the corner of his mouth.

"Mikal," he whispered, gently shaking the sleeping boy's shoulder.

"Huh!" Mikal awoke with a fright and jumped up. "What is it? What's wrong?" He wiped his mouth with the back of his hand.

"Shh!" Yazir hissed. "Nothing's wrong. Keep your voice down. It's early, father is still asleep. You were right, the looking glass is strange. It talked to me. Come and see."

"The looking glass?" Now Mikal was wide awake, a look of alarm on his face. "What do you mean it talked to you?"

"I think there's a girl trapped inside. She called my name, called for help. She woke me up. Didn't you hear her?"

Wide-eyed, Mikal slowly shook his head. "I didn't hear a thing."

Yazir grabbed him by the arm. "Come and see."

The two boys tiptoed down the hall into Yazir's room and stood before the mirror. The looking glass stood alone in the corner; chinks of sunlight high-lighting the rich red-brown colour of its timber, and their fuzzy likenesses reflected in the dull-grey glass.

Suddenly Mikal gave a soft gasp and stiffened. As they watched, their reflections became obscured as wisps of mist began to swirl within the glass.

"You've got to get rid of it," Mikal urged. "I don't like this. I think Khasis has enchanted the glass."

"Don't be such a baby, Mikal. This is wondrous. It's…" But

before Yazir could finish, he was interrupted.

"Yazir," said a girl's voice from within the looking glass. "Help me." The words were soft, seductive, compelling.

"It's her!" Yazir said. He turned excitedly to Mikal. "Hear her? She's calling my name, asking me for help."

"Sorry." Mikal slowly shook his head. "I didn't hear a thing."

Both boys peered into the looking glass. The swirling mist had thickened and filled the mirror to the point where no trace of their reflections remained. As the brothers watched, a figure began to materialise and move towards them.

"Look." Yazir saw a pretty girl emerge from the fog. She had long, curly dark hair and large brown eyes. The girl clutched a flimsy white garment around herself and cast fearful glances over her shoulder. "It's her."

Mikal frowned at his brother and peered harder into the mirror. He could definitely see a dark shape lurking in the mist, but it seemed to move with the swirls, always obscured by the thickest fog.

"I can't make her out," Mikal said.

"Yazir," the girl pleaded. "You've got to help me escape. An evil sorcerer has imprisoned me here." She pouted, her bottom lip trembling ever so slightly. "You're the only one who can help me."

"How?" Yazir said. "What can I do?"

Mikal stared at his brother in alarm, then peered back into the mirror. Every time Mikal got close to making out the dark shape, it moved, almost as though it was trying to thwart him. All he glimpsed were shadows and movements. But even so, whatever it was, he felt certain it was not a girl. He wasn't even sure it was human.

Yazir began to reach for the mirror.

"No!" cried Mikal. He struck his brother's hand away from the glass.

Yazir flinched and drew back. He licked his lips slowly, his eyes darting from Mikal to the mirror.

Mikal moved to stand between him and the mirror.

Yazir shoved Mikal out of the way.

"What's going on?" yelled their father from his bedroom. "What are you two up to?"

"You've scared her off," Yazir said. His face was red and his eyes were wild. He glared at his brother and pointed at the mirror. "She's gone!"

It was true. All Mikal could see now in the mirror was his own distorted reflection. The mist had evaporated completely.

Mikal turned to his brother. "You've got to get rid of the looking glass. I don't know what she is, but you mustn't let her out."

"You're demented," Yazir said. "You're just jealous because you can't see or hear her. Get out of my room and stay away from my looking glass."

"It's all your fault," Yazir grumbled as he shovelled another pile of horse manure from the stable floor into the barrow. "This is going to take hours."

"My fault?" Mikal threw his shovel into the muck in the barrow and stood with his hands on his hips glaring at his brother. "You start acting crazy with that cursed looking glass and you say it's my fault." He snorted. "I like that."

"You were the one who yelled first. You woke father!" Now Yazir dropped his shovel and glared back at Mikal. "And you're the one who scared the girl away."

"That's it, isn't it?" Mikal nodded knowingly to himself. "It's not so much this chore that bothers you, it's that bizarre girl in the looking glass. You're besotted by her."

"There's nothing bizarre about her," insisted Yazir. "She's just a normal girl."

"Yazir! Look at the facts. We find a sorcerer's looking glass which acts like a window into a land of mist. You have conversations with some girl who says she's trapped there. And you say she's not bizarre?"

"She's just an ordinary girl who's trapped there."

"Trapped where, Yazir? Where is she? Who is she? What's her name?" Mikal reached out and touched his brother on the arm. "There's something not right here. I can feel it."

"You don't know," Yazir said quietly. "You haven't seen her." He looked right through Mikal, picturing the girl in his mind. "She needs my help."

"She might appear to you as a pretty girl, Yazir, but she hides from me. Don't trust her. Who knows what she really is. Who knows what you'll let loose if you help her escape."

Yazir shrugged out of his brother's grasp. "She's an ordinary girl, I tell you!"

"Okay, let's assume she is an ordinary girl. Let's ask her where she is and how she got trapped in there in the first place? It shouldn't be a problem if she's hasn't got anything to hide."

Yazir shook his head.

"Come on, Yazir," Mikal said in exasperation. "I'll even muck out the stables by myself. What have you got to lose?"

"Oh, all right," Yazir said. "I'll show you." And he turned and stomped out of the stable towards the castle.

Mikal caught up to his brother at the kitchen entrance and they crept through the castle to Yazir's bedroom.

"You're not allowed to say anything," Yazir told Mikal as they stood in front of the looking glass. "You'll scare her away again. I'll talk to her and you'll just have to listen to me. Agreed?"

Mikal nodded. "What do we do now?"

"Just wait, I'm sure she knows when I'm here."

Sure enough, the mirror began to cloud over.

"Yazir?"

Her voice captivated him. "I'm here," he said.

"I'm running out of time, Yazir. It hurts me to come to you like this. You must help me escape."

"I can't see you," Yazir said.

"I'm coming."

They saw movement. For Yazir it materialised as a beautiful girl, but for Mikal she still remained an elusive shadow.

"Where are you?" Yazir asked.

"Here, Yazir, in the looking glass."

"How did you get there?"

"I'm trapped. It hurts. It hurts a lot." Yazir saw a tear trickle down her face. "You've got to help me."

"I will," Yazir said.

"What's she saying?" said Mikal. "Ask her who she is. Ask her why I can't see her?"

Yazir glared at Mikal, then turned back to the mirror. "I want to ask you some other questions…"

"It's hurting me, Yazir." There was pain in her gentle voice. "Come back to me," she pleaded. "I've got to go. Come back and set me free."

"I'll come back," Yazir promised.

The mist began to thin.

"Ask her the questions," demanded Mikal. "She's avoiding the questions."

"Shut up," said Yazir.

The mirror was clear and she was gone.

"But you haven't got any proof," persisted Mikal. "You didn't ask her the questions."

"I've got all the proof I need. You're just jealous that I'm the one she needs. I'm going to help her."

"You've got it all wrong," Mikal insisted. "I don't care about her. I'm worried what she'll do to you. You've got to get rid of the looking glass. You can't let her out."

"Just you try and stop me!"

The next morning, Yazir watched from behind his bedroom shutters as Mikal strolled out to the stable with a shovel over his shoulder. At last, he thought, smirking to himself. With Mikal now busy and their father out riding patrol with a squad of cavalry, he would be alone for at least an hour.

Yazir latched the shutters and pushed his door closed. He stood in front of the looking glass and grinned. A part of him wanted to yell out and announce his arrival to the girl, but another part of him knew all he had to do was wait.

Before long, tendrils of mist began to writhe and swirl within the mirror. Gradually Yazir's reflection began to disappear from view as mist filled the looking glass. Then he heard the girl's familiar, alluring voice.

"Yazir…?"

"I'm here," he said.

There was movement in the mist, a shape, a spray of dark hair. Then he could see her, the white fabric clutched modestly at her neck, her eyes bright with anticipation.

"You came," she said. She gave him a coy smile and fluttered her eyes. "I knew you wouldn't let me down."

Yazir shrugged and blushed slightly.

"Are you ready to help me, Yazir?" Her question was loaded with a sense of promise.

"I think so," he said, trying to ignore the small doubt niggling in the back of his mind.

Her expression suddenly darkened. "I'm relying on you, Yazir. Without your help I'm trapped here." She paused and held him with her penetrating gaze. "Will you set me free?"

"Yes," he assured her. He could feel his heart beating rapidly. "Just tell me what I have to do."

She let out a sigh of relief and her face lit up with a smile. "That's simple, Yazir." She stretched her hand out towards him. "All you have to do is reach into the looking glass and take my hand."

He reached towards the mirror, then hesitated, looking from his hand to the mirror and back again. Fleetingly he remembered his brother's warning and wondered if he was doing the right thing. In that brief moment, a look of pure malice crossed the girl's face, but she replaced it with an expression of rapt longing as he looked back again.

She nodded encouragement. He smiled back uneasily and tentatively reached into the mirror. His hand passed through the glass as though he was reaching into a pool of water.

He gasped. His heart missed a beat.

It was like thrusting his hand into ice water. Worse! It was so cold inside the mirror it seemed to burn.

She grabbed his hand.

He cried out in pain and fright. A chill ran through him and he began to shiver. The pain was almost unbearable.

"Pull, Yazir." Her eyes blazed with triumph. "Set me free!"

Yazir pulled with all his might, but the girl hardly budged. Her grip was unbearably tight and in the cold he felt as though his hand was being crushed. He tried to let go and jerk free but her grip became even tighter.

"Pull!" It was an order.

He could feel her nails digging into his flesh, breaking the skin. Yazir began to whimper in agony. "Let me go," he begged. But her grip tightened even more and he felt as though his hand was being crushed between huge slabs of masonry.

Yazir began to slip towards the mirror. His feet scrabbled for purchase on the floor. He gritted his teeth, imploring her with his eyes, but she returned his gaze with cold indifference.

"You're hurting me," he sobbed.

But her only response was a low sinister laugh, which turned to one of exultation as she began to move. Any beauty she might once have possessed was gone. Now her face was composed of cruel, hard lines, her eyes as cold as the blade of a sword.

"Pull." This time it was a shriek of triumph.

Suddenly the door behind Yazir crashed open and Mikal burst into the room. He lunged past Yazir with his dung shovel raised two-handed above his head. He smashed it down on the mirror.

There was a crash, and shards of glass exploded around them.

Yazir had felt the girl begin to pass through the mirror. But when the glass shattered, her terrible grip relaxed. He hit the floor amid a rain of glass and screwed his eyes shut, curling himself into a tight ball.

A silence followed, broken only by his great sobs.

Mikal knelt down and shook him gently. "Yazir, are you all right?"

Yazir took a couple of deep breaths and nodded. "I think so. Except for my hand." He cradled his hand to his chest and sat up. "Thank you, Mikal. What about you?"

Mikal pushed himself to his feet with the aid of his shovel and flexed his biceps like a circus strong man. "Nothing wrong with me." He grinned. "Not even a scratch."

"What about the girl?" Yazir said. "What happened to her?"

Mikal moved to the mirror's empty frame, his shoes crunching splinters of glass. "Girl, you say?" He used the blade of his shovel to poke amongst the broken pieces of mirror then stepped aside. "See for yourself."

Yazir stared in disbelief, the colour draining from his face. A severed hand lay twitching on the floor amid the shards of glass, though not the petite hand of a stranded damsel, but the four-fingered claw of some unspeakable creature. The flesh was a grey-green colour the texture of toad skin, and each finger was tipped with a dark talon.

"There's your girl," Mikal said. "Or at least part of her. Hopefully the rest of her got left behind."

Yazir noticed a thick gooey black substance dripping down the empty mirror frame to pool beneath the severed claw. He pulled a face. "Is that what I think it is?"

"Blood, you mean?" Mikal nodded and wrinkled his nose in disgust. "I'd say so, and I'm not cleaning it up. That's your part of the contract. Now let's take a look at your hand."

Yazir stood up and gingerly uncovered his injured hand. He stared at it in amazement. He had expected to find it torn and bleeding, but there was not a mark on it. "I don't understand." He could still feel the claws tearing it, still feel the terrible cold burning. "She grabbed it inside the looking glass, crushed it, gouged it…" He shook his head and flexed his fingers.

Mikal shrugged. "Maybe that happened in the looking glass world, not ours. Think yourself lucky you weren't pulled into the mirror. In that world, your hand probably is injured."

Yazir stared beyond Mikal as he re-lived the horror. "For a moment I thought she was going to drag me in there." He shuddered at the memory. "Thank God you arrived when you did. What made you come back? Did you suspect I was up to something?"

"Maybe," Mikal said with a glimmer in his eye. "Maybe I

simply decided I'd shovelled enough dung." He laughed and tossed the shovel to his still-dazed brother.

"You can use it to clean this up." Mikal waved his hand at the broken glass and mess on the floor. He put his arm around Yazir's should and squeezed him. "Then you can you use it to muck out the stables. I think it's your turn, don't you?"

The Sorcerer's Looking Glass — Afterword

Mirrors have long played a part in fantasy stories and fairy tales. Sometimes as doorways to alternate worlds or different dimensions. Other times they are not so much doorways as traps or prisons. But if that's so, who holds the keys?

The initial inspiration for this story came from thinking about these magical possibilities, and wondering what lay on the dark side of an enchanted mirror. Then the brothers Mikal and Yazir came to inhabit my mind and their story unfolded on the page before me as I wrote.

For a while it made me look askance at mirrors.

'The Sorcerer's Looking Glass' was first published in the HarperCollins anthology *Fantastic Worlds*.

Christmas Morning

In the pre-dawn darkness, a shadowy figure moved soundlessly up the driveway of the suburban brick-veneer house. It slid between the standard rose bushes bordering the drive, and crossed the lawn to take up a watchful position outside the lounge room window.

Inside, a plastic Christmas tree, hung with tinsel and shiny baubles, was illuminated with dozens of tiny coloured lights that cast a faint rainbow glimmer across the room. Under the tree were toys: dolls, two pink tricycles with white wicker baskets on their handlebars, a couple of red-felt stockings stuffed with treats, and more. All in pairs, two by two.

The figure outside stood by the window, still and silent, waiting…

Before long, two pretty young girls, identical twins about six years old, danced into the room, tittering and shushing each other. They had sleep-tousled blonde hair, wore matching pale blue pyjamas decorated with white polar bears, and their eyes were bright and alive with Christmas morning mischief and joy.

They "oohed" and "ahhed" at the tree, poked in delight at the presents, giggling and dancing as they cast skittish glances over their shoulders lest anyone should hear them.

The dark figure outside watched them intently, still as a statue, taking in their every move. After a while, a first glimmer of twilight revealed the figure as a man and he turned to grimace at the rising sun.

The girls shushed each other. The figure outside froze.

All was still and silent inside and out.

As the dawn light spread across the sky, the two girls started to fade. They quickly became translucent; their blonde hair diaphanous, their pale skin sheer as tissue paper. Their giggles became distant, faint. Soon they were gossamer, then mist…

Then they were gone.

The watcher trudged to the front door and let himself into the house.

He flopped into an armchair opposite the Christmas tree and burst into sobs. Sunlight shone into the room, illuminating him. He was a man of middling years, with angry red and mottled-yellow burn scars on his hands and face.

Eventually, now weeping quietly, he got to his feet, switched off the festive lights and began to dismantle the Christmas tree. He would pack it away along with the decorations and presents until next year. As he had done last year, and every year since his wife and daughters had died more than a decade before.

He cursed himself for having left the box of matches on the coffee table when he snuffed out the candles that Christmas Eve. Cursed himself for not having replaced the battery in the smoke alarm, and wished he had died along with his wife when they had tried to rescue their girls from the flames that terrible morning…

And he resolved to somehow get through one more year, in the hope that he might catch another glimpse of his lost girls next Christmas.

Christmas Morning — Afterword

This story was written for *Hell's Bells*, a flash fiction anthology published by the Australasian Horror Writers Association. The brief was to write a Christmas ghost story in five hundred words or less.

The Christmas ghost story has a long tradition, much older than Dickens' *A Christmas Carol*, harking back to medieval times…darker times when the Pagan Yule festival celebrated the Wild Hunt (a ghostly procession in the winter sky) and other traditions. At these times people's thoughts turned to winter, death, rebirth.

When I wrote this story, I was conscious of those traditions, but my thoughts also turned to celebration, love, loss, and regret. So I focussed the emotions that bubbled up into this chilling, heart-rending tale.

The Black Diamond of the Elephant God

ONE

I took leave of my friend Tomlinson and departed the city of Allahabad on the 12th of March 1843, bound for Banaras by palanquin on my quest. My bearers carried me along a shady dam on the right side of the Ganges until we came to a rickety bridge of boats where we crossed and headed east on a dusty, pot-holed road.

At first everything was as one would expect. We passed local peasants carrying burdens on their heads, Hindoo pilgrims, and a caravan of heavily laden carts pulled by grimy camels with bells tied around their ankles so they tinkled as they walked. The roadside was dotted with villages, pagodas, mosques and man-made pools, many shaded by pleasant groves of mangoes, tamarinds, and bananas; all of which lulled me into a false sense of complacency and left me fully unprepared for what lay ahead.

When we set out the blazing sun had been so fierce that my bearers could proceed only very slowly, but as the afternoon progressed dark grey clouds obscured the sun. As the temperature fell the bearers picked up their pace considerably, but to our surprise the sky continued to become even darker, so that by the time it should only have been evening twilight we were enveloped in darkness so impenetrable that the bearers had to light torches to illuminate our way.

Before long a wind began to buffet my palanquin, making it sway alarmingly. The bearers muttered uneasily amongst themselves. The wind gusts soon turned into a gale; rumbling thunder came closer and closer, and large drops of rain soon began to fall in such torrents that our torches were extinguished. The roadway quickly became a swamp and the bearers frequently slipped, and sometimes fell down, for they were only able to see the way when the dazzling flashes of lightning shone across their path.

"Please, Sahib, Mr Giles Freeman," the head bearer shouted over the noise of the rain. "The way is dangerous."

I nodded and ordered them to halt. The road was empty, bordered on both sides by jungle, and there was no village we could turn to for shelter. We came upon a bridge and they stumbled down beside it and set me down under its arch. I alighted from the palanquin and had to brace myself against the driving rain, the bridge overhead offering little protection. I clambered back up to the road and was looking into the storm contemplating our way forward—puzzled that such a violent, unseasonable tempest like this should have come out of nowhere—when a mighty explosion and a blinding flash knocked me to the ground.

Dazed, I clambered to my feet and there came another colossal boom. In the brilliant flash of lightning that accompanied the thunder bolt I saw the shadow of an elephant cast across the road. But this elephant seemed somehow distorted; the body shape was wrong and the ears appeared scalloped and ragged. I shot a rapid glance left then right, but of the beast there was no sign. My head filled with what sounded like many voices chanting. Then the night went dark again and the image was gone. Suddenly a loud trumpeting roar bellowed from the darkness. I should have called for my handgun, but I was frozen, held in thrall by the extraordinary occurrence.

Then there came another crash of thunder and the spell was broken. The chanting in my head ceased and I turned back towards the bridge where I could just make out the half-naked figures of my bearers crouched closely together for protection behind the palanquin. They were whimpering and keening, and in the illumination from another more distant flash of lightning I could see their eyes were wide with terror.

I shivered, feeling very cold all of a sudden, and peered back along the road and into the jungle, but whatever had been there was gone. It must have been a frightened elephant, I told myself. The peculiar creature I imagined I had seen had probably been induced by a dramatic shadow play of jungle fronds thrashing in the wind and merging with the shadow of some terrified animal. What I imagined was chanting must have been some sort of ringing in my ears caused by the boom of the thunderclap. I concluded that the work I had done translating Tomlinson's weird and wonderful Sanskrit texts had fuelled my imagination into thinking I had seen the monstrous entity described in those ancient writings.

With nothing more to be seen I returned to my palanquin and climbed inside to wait out the storm, but I remained uneasy and disconcerted by the incident. Lying there with the rain beating down, thunder booming and lightning flashing, I considered my situation. I had come to India at the behest of Tomlinson, an old university chum working for the British East India Company in Allahabad. He wrote asking me to translate a packet of ancient Sanskrit texts he had found inside a grotesque terracotta elephant idol that had been unearthed by a local well-digger in a ruinous area on the outskirts of the city.

At first I was disinclined to accept Tomlinson's invitation. I had already made a commitment to the British Museum, and, to be frank, I doubted the authenticity of his discovery. But Tomlinson had anticipated my doubt and cannily enclosed a single "page" from the find with his letter. Upon examination, it was immediately obvious to me that the remarkably preserved text, which was etched on a piece of oiled banana leaf, was indeed unique—pre-Vedic and unlike anything that had hitherto been found anywhere on the subcontinent. But what was even more fascinating was that the ancient text itself claimed to have been translated from an even more arcane Tibetan script.

I immediately dashed off an apology to the British Museum, packed my valise and set off post-haste for India, travelling to Bombay by clipper, to Delhi by horse, to Agra by camel, and to Allahabad by palanquin. Tomlinson, the good fellow, installed me there in a five-room bungalow with a wide veranda and sent a houseboy over to look after me. I immediately set myself up in the study and started work on the singular texts, and as they slowly began to reveal their esoteric secrets, I was seduced by what they contained.

The seduction was not from their numerous arcane pre-Aryan incantations and rituals, nor from the graphic descriptions of sacrifices and cannibalism performed in the name of their primeval deities—grotesquely fascinating as they were—but by the repeated references to the Black Diamond of the Elephant God. But this god was *not* the popular Hindoo deity Ganesha, rather it seemed to be a somewhat less benign elephant-headed pagan predecessor to the son of Shiva and Parvati. A deity whose name I could not translate for it seemed to be written in another language, perhaps the aforementioned mysterious Tibetan script. The Sanskrit, however, described the deity as the "Old One" and the Black Diamond of this god as the "Opener of the Way." According to my reading, the Black Diamond was in fact a massive gem, the likes of which has never been seen.

I dismissed the notion of a malignant elephant god as primitive superstition, but the possibility that such a diamond might exist was entirely plausible because the Indian mines of Golconda were rightly famous for producing magnificent diamonds—the legendary Great Mogul; the *Koh-i-Noor*, Babur's "Mountain of Light"; the *Darya-i-Noor*, the largest pink diamond in the world; and Jean-Baptiste Tavernier's French Blue, to name but a few—but even these famous diamonds could not compare to the description of the black stone of my quest.

According to Tomlinson's ancient texts, a black diamond the size of a hen's egg was said to sit upon the palm of an elephant-headed idol in a subterranean temple situated in a sacred town beside a sacred river. As vague and mysterious as these directions might have been, the interior layout of the temple and the location of the idol itself, on the other hand, were described in precise detail. As though the author was describing a real temple, a place he knew well.

As soon as I realised this I sent word to Tomlinson to come over immediately.

"Good God, old chap!" he said when I told him. "Tell me exactly what the text says."

I retrieved my notes and brought them into the drawing room where we sat across from each other on teak armchairs padded with overstuffed muslin cushions and I read the translation out aloud to him.

He frowned in disgust at the pagan rituals, hooted in delight at the description of the mighty gem, even making a joke that it was courageous of me to read the Sanskrit incantations out aloud. But he became quiet and serious when I recounted the details of the temple.

The next morning, he sent off a number of discrete enquiries, and, as luck would have it, two weeks later we received word from a friend of his by the name of Major Carpenter that in Banaras there was apparently an obscure underground temple that matched the description we had circulated.

Tomlinson insisted I leave for Banaras immediately, even though Company duties unfortunately confined him for the time being to Allahabad; hence the reason I now found myself alone, huddled in my palanquin in the dark under a bridge with a torrential thunder storm beating down. To make matters worse, a terrible feeling of foreboding and trepidation had come upon me. In my mind's eye, I kept seeing the weirdly distorted image of something elephantine. It made me recall Tomlinson's joke that my reading of the mysterious texts, my verbal utterance of the ancient incantations, might somehow open a crack between the past and the present, between our world and another realm, and allow something primeval and forgotten to gain a toehold in our world.

I waited there alone with my fanciful thoughts in the dark under the bridge for more than an hour before the storm and the lightning finally abated. When the last of the thunder died away, the starry heavens appeared without a cloud and the morning dawned bright and clear. Nature seemed to be revived; the air was fresh and aromatic, and the fields and foliage seemed to glow in the brightest hues. With a lightened heart I set off once more for Banaras.

The bearers proceeded at a good pace, and despite the delay caused by the storm they performed the whole journey of seventy-five miles in less than twenty-four hours; for at 12 o'clock on the following day we reached the outskirts of the city where we were met by Major Carpenter's servant sent to guide us to his bungalow.

When the big, burly man shook my hand I trusted him straight away by the direct way he stared into my eyes. He was an old-school East India Company man with a big smile and an even bigger greying moustache, who had survived the devastating cholera pandemic and stayed on in India regardless.

That evening after a dinner of mild goat curry and fragrant spiced rice, we sat on rattan chairs on the veranda to talk, smoke, and sip on gin and tonics. We were in a fenced cantonment. Opposite us were the bungalows of other officers and beyond those the troop barracks.

A house boy pulled on a cord to work the horizontal *punkah* fans above us to waft cooling air and help keep the mosquitoes at bay.

"So why are you looking for this temple?" Major Carpenter asked.

I hesitated. "It's an anthropological expedition."

I made no mention of the Black Diamond. The reason for this was two-fold. The first was that it sounded farfetched, and I did not want the Major to think I was crazy. The second was that if the mythical gemstone was real, I wanted to keep it secret.

He nodded. "These Indians have an ancient culture. A lot of it is already lost. I think it's decent that chaps like you study and record it for posterity."

"I enjoy my work," I said.

Carpenter lit a cheroot and puffed on it. "I have arranged for my aid, Captain Rogers, to take you to the temple tomorrow."

I tipped my glass to him. "Thank you, Major."

"Rogers is a good chap, knows the natives hereabout like the back of his hand. You will be safe with him."

TWO

Captain Rogers was waiting for me the next morning after breakfast, but rather than wearing his distinctive red company uniform he was dressed in local garb; pyjama style home-spun cotton pants, a loose collarless kurta shirt, and a turban of all things.

In response to my look of puzzlement he said, "Good morning, Freeman. I have a set for you as well. It will be better if we dress like locals, easier to gain access to the temple."

"But what about my notes?" I gestured at my satchel. "I might need them."

"Put them in this," he said, handing me a simple calico bag with a shoulder strap. "It's what the natives use."

"We are white, Rogers, we are not going to pass for locals."

"Yes, but we might pass as acclimatised foreigners rather than *firangi*. I can speak a smattering of Pashto and Hindi, and I have been here so long this damned sun has cooked my skin, so we might even pass for Pathans. Either way, for this venture it's better to dress like this than to look like Company men."

So, at his behest I changed clothes, donned the shoulder bag and we made our way on foot towards the busy old part of the city. We soon found ourselves traversing dusty, narrow and crooked streets lined with tall houses; mud brick on the lower levels and timbered on the upper levels, four and five storeys high. They came in a variety of colours—eggshell-blue, mould stained white-wash, weathered silver-grey timber, and sandstone yellow—ornamented with verandas, carved latticed windows, and fretwork galleries running around each storey.

The streets became even more constricted with people and animals the farther we penetrated the city, until eventually we were navigating filthy alleys so narrow and confined that there was scarcely room for us to squeeze past the holy cows that seemed to wander the city unopposed, munching on whatever rubbish or offerings they could find. These laneways were fouled not only with their dung, but also that of goats, dogs, and even human excrement, so the place smelled ripe with decay and pestilence. I shuddered to think of the ravages that would occur if the cholera or small pox, or a fire, were to break out in these close, narrow places.

We entered a busy bazaar ahum with many voices, the cluck of caged fowl and the bleat of penned goats. We shouldered our way through the crowds while Hindoo and Mussulman stall holders offered us clay cups of hot, spicy chai; freshly baked flat breads; sticks of aromatic incense; and sacred collars composed of horn, ivory, and flowers. Mingling there in the throng were a great many Hindoo devotees; numerous lame and blind persons; a half-naked ash-smeared *sadhu*, a holy-man, wrapped in a mangy leopard skin and carrying an enormous trident; and crowds of the most impudent beggars.

Beyond the bazaar we entered another quarter of the city where wily harlots came to the lattices or onto the galleries and endeavoured to attract our attention. My inclination was to ignore these women and press on, but to my astonishment Rogers halted and waved at one of the balconies.

I glanced up in time to see one of the gaily clad women return his greeting. "What are you doing?" I said.

"We'll wait here for my, ah, friend to join us."

"Your friend? But these women are prostitutes," I exclaimed.

Rogers glared at me and for a moment I thought he might strike me.

"Sorry, old chap," I continued. "I didn't mean —"

"These women are not whores," he snapped. "They are *bayaderes*, *devadasis*, temple dancers."

I nodded, recognising the Sanskrit roots of the latter name; *deva* meaning god or goddess and *dasi* meaning female servant. But I also knew that these women sold their favours in the name of their deity and that Banaras had a reputation for training some of the most beautiful and alluring *bayaderes* in the land. Indeed, it is said that there are young women from this revered city dedicated to temples in the most distant provinces of the empire where they spend their days dancing, performing temple duties, and engaging in a succession of fleeting, transient paid amours.

Before I could do little more than nod, the woman I had spied on the balcony burst from the doorway, rushed up to Rogers in a swirl of pale-blue silk and threw her arms around his neck, the rows of thin silver and enamelled bracelets on her wrists rattling with the gesture.

"This is Sreevani," Rogers said by way of introduction.

She turned her gaze to me and I saw that she was indeed a strikingly handsome woman. She had a fair complexion for an Indian, nicely proportioned features, long dark eyelashes and enormous brown, kohl-ringed eyes that gleamed with a coquettish sparkle. She pressed the palms of her hands together and bowed her head. "*Namaste*," she said.

"Sreevani will guide us," Roger's added.

"*Namaste*," I replied to her. "My name is Giles, Giles Freeman. Do you speak English? Do you know the temple I seek?"

She wobbled her head in that confounded Indian manner, which I took to mean yes.

"Will you take us there?" I asked.

Sreevani turned her face away and would not meet my gaze.

"Sreevani?" Rogers prompted. When she remained silent, he turned to me and said, "I should tell you, Freeman, Sreevani did not want to take us to this temple. She says it's a bad place. She's only doing this at my insistence."

When Sreevani finally looked up I recognised pain in her expression, sadness in her beautiful eyes. She said, "My younger sister was dedicated to the place you seek, the temple of the Old One. I know where it is."

Then she turned without further explanation and set off with Rogers and myself in tow, leaving the good-humoured jibes and catcalls of her *bayadere* sisters behind, and I was left to wonder at her reluctance to guide us to the temple.

She led us towards the river, through an even narrower maze of lanes that she called *galis*, so closely encompassed with buildings that we were obliged to walk single file. But I was barely concentrating on our surroundings. My stomach was aflutter with anticipation and I wanted to break into a run. This was the culmination of weeks of work and if we were lucky, I would soon know if the Black Diamond was real. We passed numerous Hindoo pagodas, shrines and places of prayer, before finally arriving at an unremarkable stone edifice where a series of masonry steps led down to a dark portico.

"This is the place," she said. "Wait here."

My heart pounded as I watched her descend. At the bottom, she was halted by a white-robed acolyte who had stepped out of the shadows to bar her way. She engaged him in a local dialect, baksheesh provided to her by myself for the purpose changed hands, and she returned with the man to collect us.

"No touch," he said in gruff, heavily accented English. "Just looking."

We nodded agreement and the acolyte conducted us down the steps into the cool, dark interior of the temple where we found a deep pool of dirty, green water surrounded by a wall of hewn stone and fretwork. I was breathing fast and perspiring, because I knew immediately that this was indeed the place I sought. Every feature was exactly as described in the ancient writings, even down to the huge block of granite beside the pool which the texts had described as a sacrificial altar. As my gaze fell on it I was disconcerted to see it was stained with a coagulated dark substance.

We made our way into a large open area. The temple was cavernous—deceptively large given its small entrance—hollowed out under the ancient city above. Despite the stagnant temple pool and the proximity of the Ganges River, the air was dry, desiccated, and smelled of dust and dung. Its furthest reaches were shrouded in gloom. I glanced back the way we had come.

On a masonry bench by the wall of the pool sat an aged little man, clearly not of Indian stock by the look of his Asiatic eyes, and when he smirked I had the fleeting impression his teeth had been filed into points. At his side stood a naked fakir whose hair hung like ropes from his head to his knees, and who had painted his body and face in such a strange and hideous manner that I could not take my eyes off him. He appeared to answer my curious gaze with scorn and contempt.

We moved into the main interior of the temple, past several small, dark grottoes or transepts used for worship, which were dimly lighted by oil lamps. Ahead was the stone structure of the *sanctum sanctorum*, what the Hindoos would call the *garbha gruha* or "womb chamber". It was the largest edifice in the temple, set further back and apart from the chambers, where their god, hewn in stone, was said to reside. Here too everything in the temple was exactly as described in those ancient writings, so all that remained for me to do was to confirm the deity's presence and whether or not it held the Black Diamond.

I tried to swallow the lump in my throat, but my mouth was dry. Sacred cows and calves were standing about in several apartments as we approached the chamber, but in one room we unexpectedly found a pair of these holy animals lying dead upon the floor. Such a thing seemed incongruous in a land that revered these creatures and I wanted to take a closer look, but the pestilential smell was overbearing so we quickly moved on. I glanced back at the old man with his naked attendant and got the impression they were sneering and smirking at us.

Then, we stepped into the opening of the inner sanctum, and came upon the massive stone idol of the nameless Elephant God.

Rogers gasped and Sreevani clutched his arm.

"Good lord," I said, going weak at the knees. "It's real!" I gaped at it in awe.

Carved from a single slab of pitted grey granite, it was perched imposingly on a dais of polished black onyx. Mottled and weather-beaten, it was both repulsive and compelling at the same time. I could hardly take my eyes off it even though the very sight of the thing filled me with loathing and disgust. It sat in a lotus position—like a malignant meditative Ganesha—with both hands, for it too had human hands, resting together palms upward on its chubby, all too human, crossed legs. But the grotesque elephantine head dispelled any possibility of humanity, with its webbed, tentacle-fringed ears, its twisted, crystalline tusks and its cold, wicked-looking eyes.

An icy fear knotted my bowels. I lowered my gaze, unable to hold its stony stare.

Offerings had been placed before the deity, but instead of the usual flowers, sweets, and milk, I observed prickly, nettle-like herbs, the carcass of a rat, and a brass pot containing a ruby red liquid that looked suspiciously like blood, and perhaps profanely explained the stains on the sacrificial altar and the dead cows we had seen. The tableau was like a dark parody of an altar in a Hindoo temple, but everything was corrupted, wrong. Even the incense smoke that wreathed the idol exuded not the familiar sweet scent of sandalwood, but a bitter, coppery odour that made my eyes water.

I lifted my gaze and it was irresistibly drawn to the black jewel resting in the palms of the idol's hands. Surely it couldn't be genuine, it was too big… But if it were real, how much would it be worth back in England? Everything else in the text had proved correct and there it was, right before my eyes, every bit as magnificent as I had imagined, its strangely angled polished facets glinting in the flickering lamp light. I stared at the diamond, mesmerised, and felt a dizzy swoon as the very air began to shimmer and distort. Then I heard the sound of many voices chanting, like a monotonously intoned canticle, similar to that which I had heard on the road from Allahabad. I glanced from Rogers to Sreevani but, rather peculiarly, they appeared oblivious to the voices.

All of a sudden I was struck with an overwhelming desire to take hold of the diamond. I tried to resist, remembering my promise to the acolyte at the entrance not to touch anything, but a soothing thought in my head urged me forward, telling me there was no harm. When I tried to dismiss the idea, it returned with redoubled intensity and I was unable to disregard the urge.

I reached out and grasped hold of the Black Diamond…

The great gem felt icy cold, and as I held it a chill crawled up my arm. The chanting voices in my head suddenly fell expectantly silent and I looked up to see the idol's eyes snap open and its stone form turn to living, reeking flesh.

"Oh, dear God!" I gasped. What blasphemous phenomenon was this?

I lurched backwards in fear and revulsion, then froze as the creature pinned me with its piercing bloodshot yellow eyes. The noisome, carrion stink of its breath washed over me as it regarded me with a frosty glare of contempt. Then its chilling gaze moved from me to Rogers and it threw back its enormous head and let out a hideous trumpeting roar that resounded through the chamber.

Was I hallucinating again? I turned to Rogers and Sreevani and their looks of terror confirmed they were witnessing what I was seeing. The creature was alive.

Released from its gaze I stumbled backwards and collided with Sreevani. She steadied me and the three of us ran from the chamber. The earthen floor shook as the loathsome behemoth stomped out after us. I glanced back and saw that Rogers had come to a halt, stricken with shock. The beast's trunk snaked out towards him and I watched in horror as it latched moray-eel-like onto his face. Blood spurted in a wide arc.

I stopped and turned back.

"We cannot help him," Sreevani shrieked. "We have to get out of here."

Instinctively I grabbed for my caplock pistol, only to realise I was unarmed. I would have shot this monster point blank in the face. But it was too late, Rogers was already a limp mass of blood and gore.

I grabbed Sreevani's hand and we fled towards the exit. Behind us there came a disgusting sucking, bubbling, slurping noise and I shuddered to think what might be happening. Inside my head the ethereal chanting started again, this time discordant and frenzied. I looked down and realised dimly that I was still clutching the diamond tightly in my fist, my entire arm now completely numb from its icy touch.

Sreevani stumbled as we approached the steps leading up and out of that profane place. I turned to help her and saw the monstrous deity incarnate release what was left of Rogers, his now shrunken, bloodied body crumpling like a discarded empty sack, and an unsettling silence fell over the chamber.

I knew the creature had seen us but I dared not look directly at the thing again, for I feared the power of its piercing gaze. Then a furious trumpeting bellowed through the temple and from the corner of my eye I half saw, half sensed, the mammoth fiend start in our direction.

I had to do something but I couldn't think what. I somehow knew the answer was tucked away in the back of my mind, but the fog in my brain was making it difficult to recall. The more I tried to focus, the more the chanting in my head seemed to scramble my thinking. I looked down in despair and my gaze fell again on the diamond in my hand. The sight of the gem triggered a dim notion, and in response I dropped it into the calico bag still hanging from my shoulder.

In that instant the monstrous roaring stopped, and we plunged through the door into daylight. In the stairwell outside there was no sign of the acolyte and we leapt up the stone steps without a backward glance. Behind us the aged little man with sharpened teeth and the naked fakir with the hideously painted face yelled what sounded like obscenities at us.

THREE

We ran down one lane and along another, past the many tiny temples and shrines, bumping and jostling passers-by without a second thought until finally we emerged from the *galis* and slowed, gasping for breath.

"*Rogers...*" I panted; the gravity of what had happened now striking home as the miasma fogging my brain began to lift.

Sreevani started to weep, then lowered her head and began to pummel my chest with her fists, but I paid her little heed. We were being followed. I peered back the way we had come but could not detect any sign of pursuit, nevertheless, some sixth sense told me there was someone, or *something*, following us.

"I think we are still in danger," I said. "We have to get away."

Sreevani sobbed and kept hitting me. "This happened to my sister."

"Come on, snap out of it. We have to move. I need you to guide us."

The seriousness of what I was saying dawned on her and she stopped crying and pummelling me, sniffed a couple of times, and began to lead us back again through another area of the *galis*. I followed, but kept glancing back because the feeling we were being stalked continued unabated, prickling at the back of my neck. But it was not until we were some way from the temple that my suspicion was confirmed. I looked back as we were turning a corner and caught a glimpse of something; a flicker of movement, a fleeting shadow, and I felt both vindicated and afraid.

We *were* being followed.

I grabbed Sreevani by the arm, put the fingertips of my other hand against her soft lips to quiet her, and pressed my back against the wall adjoining the corner of the lane, motioning her to follow suit. Then I edged back to the corner and cast a surreptitious glance back the way we had come in the hope of spying who, or what, was stalking us.

At first it seemed I was mistaken, but then my vigilance was rewarded as I saw something zigzag from one patch of sunlight to another, and I recognised our pursuer for what it was.

We were being followed by a *shadow*.

Not the shadow of the Elephant God that had appeared to me in the storm on the road to Banaras, but the shadow of a short, thin man. A shadow that existed without any physical body to cast it.

A jolt of panic hit me. I half choked trying to catch my breath and my hands began to tremble. I grabbed Sreevani and ran. We careered through the narrow streets. I kept looking back to see if we were making good our escape, but if anything, the shadow was gaining on us.

"What is wrong, Giles-sahib?" Sreevani asked, infected with my fear.

I halted a moment to catch my breath. "There." I pointed. "A shadow following us. See it?"

Sreevani clutched my arm, but I pulled free and gave her a shove. "Go!" I yelled. "Run!" And I turned back to face the shadow.

It was near now, very near, only a dozen yards and closing. I could see it clearly for the first time and realised that unlike a normal shadow, it was comprised of three-dimensional details. It was the figure of a small, naked man. It leered at me showing teeth filed to points and strode purposefully towards me.

I braced my feet resolutely and waited…

And the shadow suddenly vanished; simply disappeared before my very eyes. I blinked and looked again, but there was no sign of it.

"It's gone," I called to Sreevani, who had only gone a few paces.

She wobbled her head and pointed at the sky. A large dark cloud had blotted out the sun, erasing our shadows with its own. She beckoned me to follow. "Quickly, this way, the sacred river, Mother Ganges—*Ma Ganga*—will protect us. We must follow her to the temple."

We turned towards the river, the shadow lost behind us in the sunless gloom. But when we finally burst out onto the steps, the *ghats*, that lead down to the shoreline, the sun emerged from behind the cloud, casting our shadows jaggedly across the broad stone stairs. We ran down to the water's edge where Sreevani quickly engaged a *bidi*-smoking boat wallah to take us down river. I cast an anxious glance back the way we had come, and then clambered aboard the man's aged row boat. He pushed off from the bank and manoeuvred his craft into the current.

For a moment, I thought we were safe.

Then I caught sight of the dreaded shadow again, still relentlessly pursuing us, making its way down the *ghats*. Even then I hoped the river would stop it. But the shadow barely even paused when it reached the river.

"Christ!" I swore; then grimaced wryly, because the damnable thing was walking on water.

Sreevani saw it too, striding along the surface of the river behind us, and urged the boatman to hurry.

The man turned, saw the apparition, and gave a yelp. He redoubled his efforts to row away.

"It must want the Black Diamond," I said.

I reached into my bag and took hold of the ice-cold black jewel. Suddenly the otherworldly chanting I had heard in the subterranean temple began again inside my head. Somehow touching the diamond was opening the way, connecting me to the worshippers of the nameless Elephant God and their deity. Then, as if to prove my theory, the frightful figure of the elephantine creature started to materialise right there in the air above our boat.

The boatman gave a full-throated shriek and collapsed backwards into the bow of the boat.

Sreevani slapped the diamond from my hand, and as the gem fell back into the calico bag the Elephant God apparition vanished and the air above the boat returned to normal.

I stared at Sreevani in alarm and she returned my gaze with equal trepidation. She reached down to the boat wallah and helped him up, reassuring him with calm words. He was staring at us both in wide-eyed disbelief.

The Sanskrit texts had described the gem as the "Opener of the Way", and I began to see what the phrase actually meant. I thought about tipping the stone into the river, but worried that such an act might create even more problems. I had a suspicion that the diamond might need to be returned to the underground temple in order to set things right.

The boat wallah looked around. His eyes bulged and he started yelling in Hindi. He pointed back the way we had come, leaped to the oars and began to row furiously. The shadow was rapidly closing the distance between us.

I surveyed the shore for help. The *ghats* on the river bank, which ran far down into the river, were crowded with people who stood on the steps by the hundreds, bathing, or pouring the sacred water over themselves. I could hear the sounds of ceremonial conch shells and horns being blown. Then the scene on the riverbank darkened as another large cloud blotted out the sun and the shadows faded.

Our pursuer started to fall behind and then faded away.

I sat back in the boat and took a breath. Further along the bank, there rose the flames of the funeral pyres of the recently deceased, and above the *ghats* the shore was lined with fine pagodas, sanctuaries and palaces, which rose in high terraces from the top of the steps. Lamps were kindled in front of many of these buildings, and Brahmins and devotees were gathered around the consecrated places.

But before I could spy any form of nearby help or sanctuary, the sun came out and the shadow reappeared, moving quickly towards us. Before long it was very close, so close that I could once again see its features. I still did not know how a shadow could have features, but it was sneering at me, grinning with its sharpened teeth. At last, I recognised it for what it was; kin to the wizened old man in the subterranean temple. Perhaps even the same man, for the likeness was striking.

Sreevani directed the boat wallah towards the bank and we leaped ashore even before the boat had properly landed. We scurried up the *ghats* to the surprise of the pilgrims crowding around the holy Brahmins sitting under large palm-leaf thatched umbrellas.

"The temple is close," she gasped.

"So is the shadow," I said.

We stumbled blindly towards the temple. I risked another glance behind. The shadow was almost upon us, barely three or four yards at our rear.

When we reached the temple, Sreevani halted in the entrance to pull off her slippers and indicated that I must do the same. Heaven forbid, I thought, and wrenched off my sandals.

And the shadow touched me...

FOUR

A dizzy, nauseating sensation washed over me. Everything around me began to spin in a giddying blur of broken, swirling images. I fell to my knees, gagging on bitter bile, and the very ground seemed to shift beneath me, swallowing me up.

Suddenly I found myself walking across a vast windswept plain. It was night but I could see quite clearly by the sickly light from a full moon. I was being accompanied, nay, I was being *guarded*, by a pack of creatures I could only describe as sub-human. They walked upright like men when they chose, although many simply bounded on their hands and feet, but that was where any similarity with humans ended. For they were yellow-skinned and had no faces. Their heads were smooth and featureless; no eyes, ears, nose or mouth, yet somehow they howled and mewed as they went.

I knew this had to be an hallucination... Unless the shadow had somehow transported me to another place and time. In either case, the situation should have been ominous and terrifying, but I felt remarkably calm. Subconsciously I was screaming. But it was as though I was drugged, as though false emotions, false thoughts were superimposed over my own.

The creatures shepherded me up onto a stony mound and forced me to my knees before the stone idol of the Elephant God. It was a similar statue to the one in the temple in Banaras, but this one was heavily mottled and pitted by the elements, and in the moonlight it took on a greenish hue. Its stone eyes were closed, but its body seemed to vibrate with anticipation.

Dark figures cavorted around the idol. They began to chant in an ancient language, unknown to me yet somehow I understood their words. They closed in and revealed themselves as small, dark-skinned people with black eyes and teeth filed into points. Their song, if it can be called such, beseeched the deity to accept me as its servant. To take me, feed on my life force, but hold my essence in the form of a shadow. Trap me between life and death to act as its servant.

I thought less that I had lost my mind and more that I had been transported to another dimension; that I was doomed here and I would never be able to return to Sreevani and the Ganges. My mind was racing and I thought I was going to die. I tried to run but my muscles were paralysed. But again, these thoughts and feelings were blanketed, held in check by a calm, reverential acceptance.

When the moon reached its zenith and the chanting its fever pitch, the tentacles fringing the beast's ears began to twitch and coil. Suddenly the stone idol turned to flesh and its hideous fetid breath belched over me.

Then the idol's eyes snapped open, seized on me, and the serpentine trunk snaked out and latched onto my face. In that split second I recalled with vivid clarity what had happened to Captain Rogers in the temple; saw his blood spurt and guts sucked out, saw his shrunken, desiccated body crumple as it was discarded. I tried to scream but the sound was siphoned out of me along with my eyes and blood. The pain was extraordinary, unbearable, and as my life force was drained from me I surrendered myself, resigned to serving the deity into eternity, relinquishing my status as a *Tcho-Tcho* shaman to take on the mantle of a shadow servant.

I came to my senses. I was lying on the riverside steps. Sreevani was crying and shaking my shoulders. What the hell was a *Tcho-Tcho* shaman? Where had that thought, that knowing, come from?

Dear God, I had re-lived the memories of the shadow man who had touched me. With this realisation, the otherworldly chanting that filled my head faded, my vision cleared, and my balance returned. I clambered to my feet, blinked, and looked about.

"What happened?" Sreevani said. "You were chanting in another language."

I shook my head. "I was somewhere else. Where is the shadow?"

She gasped, put one hand over her mouth, and pointed with the other.

"What?" I looked down. The shadow that had been pursuing us had now replaced my own.

Sreevani screamed. She stamped and kicked at the shadow. My heart was hammering and I broke out into a cold sweat. I took off and ran wildly along the *ghats*, yelling for help, but the shadow came with me. People were staring, backing away. I halted, panting, and Sreevani caught up.

"Quickly, follow me," she said. "We have to go to the temple. It is your only hope."

I felt compelled to grab the diamond, to take it from my calico bag and join in the romp taking place sometime in our pre-history on an arid plain somewhere high in a lofty mountain range, but I was still enough in control of my faculties to resist. The effort, however, made my head feel like it would explode.

"Giles, stop!" Sreevani yelled. "What is happening? You are chanting again."

I could hear her, but felt powerless, unable to answer. I could feel the shadow man possessing me, taking hold of my mind. But I resisted. I fought with every ounce of resolve I could muster.

Sreevani grabbed my arm and dragged me back to the temple. "He is possessed," she said as we entered, breaking into rapid Hindi. Several Hindoos conducted us quickly through dark, narrow passages to the inner sanctum, to the idol of Shiva, the five faces of his avatar lighted with religious oil lamps. Devotees were worshipping, listening to a fakir recite Sanskrit prayers in a low voice while standing on one leg and holding his right hand elevated. But I paid the man little heed because the lights from the lamps cast a shadow, and as they did I felt compelled to reach into my bag for the Black Diamond...

I could not resist.

But a strong hand gripped my neck and stopped me.

I turned violently and tried to pull free. I peered at the man who held me through a migraine blur and recognised my assailant as a Brahmin priest.

The priest pointed to my shadow, or I should say the shadow that had replaced my own, visible in the flickering lamp light, and spat the name "*Tcho-Tcho!*" I recognised it as the name of the cavorting worshippers I had "visited" after the shadow touched me—the name they had called themselves. That was what this demon shadow was called. He was the *Tcho-Tcho* shaman whose memory I had endured.

Sreevani talked hurriedly to the Brahmin priest, weeping and gesticulating, as he hustled me into a dark chamber and pulled a heavy curtain shut behind us, blackening the room. I collapsed onto cushions on the floor and my senses began to return. My breathing returned to normal as something let go of my mind.

Thank goodness for the dark. I could no longer see or feel the shadow. Relief washed over me. Like a child who sticks its head under the covers, for the moment I felt safe, even if it was a delusion. Sreevani sat down beside me and I could feel her leg against mine, hear her anxious breathing.

"What in God's name are these *Tcho-Tcho*?" I asked.

The priest squatted in front of me. "A loathsome race of half-men, who invaded India in ancient times from a mountain plateau in remote Tibet."

"Half-men? What do you mean?"

"You are possessed by the shadow of a *Tcho-Tcho* shaman in service to the Old One."

"Will it kill me?" I asked, heart pounding. "Am I going to die?"

Sreevani's hand found mine and squeezed it.

"Not yet and hopefully not at all," he said in a reassuring tone.

"Is there a way to get rid of it?"

He sighed and settled himself on the cushions on the other side of me. "That depends. I will try to help you."

"I've never heard of these *Tcho-Tcho*, never encountered anything about them in my anthropological studies."

"I'm not surprised," the priest said. "You will not find reference to them in your university text books or your theology books. Not even here in India in the *Vedas*, the *Upanishads* or the *Mahabharata*, for that matter."

"Then how do you know about them?"

"The tale of the coming of the *Tcho-Tcho* has been passed down among the Banaras Brahmins from generation to generation. My grandfather told me blood-curdling tales about them when I was just a boy. The *Tcho-Tcho* are cannibals who came to Banaras at a time when the city was still named Kashi. They tried to enslave the people of the town, poison the holy waters of *Ma Ganga*, and give their foul deity dominion over the entire land. But thankfully my ancestors were able to drive them out of this holy place."

I wished I could see his face, his body language. I listened for any inflection in his voice, trying to work out if he was telling the truth, if I could trust him.

"What happened to the *Tcho-Tcho*? Where did they go?"

"The good men of Kashi drove them east, then pursued them south down through the land you now call Burma, but lost them deep in the jungles of the Far East. Good riddance. But it seems my ancestors did not eradicate them completely from Kashi, as you now know, to your misfortune."

The priest reached out and squeezed my shoulder. "My name is Shankar," he said. "I am the head priest of this temple. Sreevani has asked me to help you but I need more information. Will you tell me how this malignant shadow came to possess you, and what dark object you have in the bag you carry, for I sense great evil."

"You are head priest here? But your English is almost perfect."

"And why not? I studied at Eton."

"You studied at Eton!" I blurted.

"Yes. I was companion to the son of a wealthy Maharaja. We went to Eton together."

"And you came back here to be a Hindoo fakir?"

"Fakir is not the correct term, old chap." He laughed. "I am what you might call a seeker of divine knowledge. It was my calling, you might say."

"The irony is that I too am a seeker of knowledge," I said. "Esoteric knowledge."

I introduced myself and recounted briefly what had happened—the text I had translated, the visitation on the journey to Banaras, the incident in the temple, the Black Diamond, and how the shadow had stalked us—answering all his questions with candour.

"I'm sorry I did not know of you to seek your help earlier instead of blundering around like a colonial buffoon," I said. "I rue the day I ever translated and read those ancient writings out."

"You read this text aloud?" Shankar said. I sensed him recoil in the dark.

"Many times. I read it out to myself to compare and verify my translation. Why, I even read parts of it to entertain my friend, Tomlinson."

"I have heard tell of this text," he said pensively. "But I will not utter its name. It is an accursed book. We believe that to speak aloud the words it contains is to invoke the malevolent ancient magic of the Old Ones."

My mouth went dry. Dear God, I thought, what have I unwittingly done to myself? "You think this is what has happened to me?"

"Yes," he said flatly.

I gripped Sreevani's small fingers tightly in mine. Her bangles clinked.

"What can I do?" I whispered.

He sighed. "I don't know yet."

Was I going to be stuck with this shadow forever? Until it took complete control of me and opened the way for the malignant Elephant God to return? I knew it was there inside me. Was it planning and plotting my overthrow?

"Can the shadow hear us?"

"Good question. No one knows."

"What if I took the diamond back to the temple?"

"If you could, it might make matters worse."

"What do you mean, if I could?"

"Give me your bag," he said.

"My bag?"

"Yes, give it to me. Just for a moment."

I pulled my hand from Sreevani's and clenched my fists. "That's ridiculous," I said, my voice rising.

"Hand it to me," he said more sternly.

I half heard, half sensed him move towards me in the dark and I snatched the bag protectively to my chest.

"See," he said mildly. "You can't give it up."

Was it too late for me, I wondered? Had I lost my free will? Was I now just an instrument of this monstrous shadow?

"Dear God! What can I do?"

"You must avoid the light. Any light." He took my hand in his, his grip firm and reassuring. "And whatever you do, do *not* touch the diamond."

"But I have to find a way to get free of the shadow."

"I will seek guidance from a learned Brahmin scholar," he said. "He has some esoteric texts that might help. But it will take time. Meanwhile, wait here until night."

I felt like a huge weight had been lifted from me. There was a glimmer of hope and I knew now I did not have to face the challenge alone.

"When it is dark Sreevani will take you to her apartment; she told me she has a room without windows. You can stay there safely until you hear from me. I will have men go with you to extinguish the lights along the way. The more the shadow is cast, the more power it will gain over you. The light of the moon and stars will still empower the shadow man. You must resist."

He left me then. I waited with Sreevani in the pitch black of the curtained alcove, curled up on the cushions, cradling my head on her bosom.

When night had fallen, Shankar returned as promised with three men. "It's time to go," he said. "But first we must ask Lord Shiva for help."

"But I am not a Hindoo," I said.

"Do you believe in God, Giles?" he asked.

I shrugged helplessly. "Sometimes."

"Then think of my faith as simply another path to God."

With that Shankar guided me back out into the temple where all but one lamp, which itself was burning with only the lowest of flames, had now been extinguished. Even so, I felt the *will* of the shadow pressing down on me, reinforced by faint echoes of *Tcho-Tcho* chanting in my ears, urging me take hold of the diamond. But by concentrating on the sounds of the temple—a priest chanting a mantra to show his adoration for Shiva, the ring of devotional bells echoing in the chamber—I was able to dispel the phantom voices and force the compulsion back into an empty corner of my mind.

I was afraid, terribly afraid. But I reminded myself I was a strong-willed, intellectual, scientific man of the West. And if I could remain strong, surely I could hold this so-called *Tcho-Tcho* shaman at bay.

We came to a fountain and performed the necessary ablutions by washing our hands and faces, then moved to an alcove where a pair of priests sat cross-legged, one before a highly adorned and garlanded statue of Ganesha, the "Remover of Obstacles," and the other before a time-blackened *lingam*, the phallus of Shiva. Many times in my life I had described myself as an atheist, and now here I was begging for mercy from pagan gods. Would a god I did not believe in help me?

I knelt in supplication with the palms of my hands pressed together to first ask Ganesha, Shiva's elephant-headed son, for help, and began intoning the mantras as instructed:

Om Gam Ganpataye Namah
Om Vignanaashnay Namah...

When many mantras had been said, and our prayers to both gods were completed, I got to my feet and made to leave. But Shankar pressed his hand against my chest.

"There is one more thing I have not told you about the *Tcho-Tcho*," he said.

Oh, Christ. "What now?"

"I have been wrestling with my conscience as to whether I should tell you, but I think perhaps it is best that you know."

"Spit it out, man."

"I have heard tell of a *Tcho-Tcho* legend that says one day a foreigner, a white man, will come and set their blasphemous god free." He peered hard into my face in the faint light. "I hope you are not that man, Giles."

I swallowed, suppressing the ever-present and growing desire to take hold of the diamond. "So do I," I said through clenched teeth. "God give me strength, so do I."

FIVE

We stepped out into the night and I immediately began to tremble with the effort of resisting the will of the shadow.

Two of the men Shankar had assigned to us ran ahead, and I observed the lights go out, one by one, as they knocked on doors and spoke with stall holders ahead of us. The third man, somewhat larger in stature than the others and hefting a stout cudgel, stayed with us as we navigated the dark lanes, following close behind, though whether to protect me or watch me, I could not tell.

Would he kill me if I succumbed to the shadow, I wondered? I waited for the blow to the back of my head. Sweat broke out on my back and forehead. I doggedly put one foot after the other, and focused all my energy on holding the chanting in my head and the will of the shadow at bay.

When we were safely ensconced in Sreevani's darkened apartment the men left us. Sreevani guided me to a *charpoy*, a rope bed, in the corner of the room, and pulled me down onto it beside her. She began to sob softly. I took her in my arms and she slipped her own dainty arms around me. We held and comforted each other for a long time. Our touches turned to caresses and we made love.

I felt safe there in the dark with her, comforted and cherished. We had only known each other a short time but she had risked everything for me. And now she gave of herself freely, with tenderness and affection. Perhaps even with love.

I thought about my predicament until I fell asleep in her arms.

When I woke, I heard Sreevani moving about the dark room.

"What are you doing?" I asked.

"It is morning. I am going to the temple to pray."

"I need you to go to Major Carpenter's bungalow and get my handgun."

I heard her gasp. She knelt down next to me and took my hand.

"Why?" she asked. "Why do you need a gun? A gun is no good against a shadow man."

"Just in case."

"In case of what?"

I thought for a moment, wondering what to tell her, how to convince her.

"You heard what your priest Shankar said."

Sreevani remained silent.

"It's hopeless. You must see that. I can't rid myself of the Black Diamond because it has a hold of me, and I can't keep resisting the shadow. I can feel the blighter getting stronger. Even here in the dark I can feel him in the back of my mind, watching, waiting, biding his time." I shuddered at the memory of his savage lust.

"Help will come, Giles-sahib," Sreevani whispered.

I shook my head. "I don't think so. There's only one way out."

"No!" she cried. "You must wait here until I bring news from the temple."

Her insistence took me aback. It was nothing unusual for an English woman to speak to a man like this, but for a Hindoo woman to speak to any man like this, let alone a man of the British Raj, was almost unheard of.

Her lack of deference, her scorn of the accepted social and cultural hierarchy, could only mean one thing. That she had strong feelings for me, and I had to admit, I felt the same for her.

I sighed. "If the shadow man gets control of me, Sreevani, he will use me to unleash the Old One on the people of this city."

She stifled a sob.

"We can't let that happen. That's why I need the pistol. And I need your help to get it."

She was silent for a moment and when finally she spoke it was in measured tones. "You wait here. First I will go to the temple for help, then I will try to get your gun."

"All right," I said. It was always possible Shankar had learned something to help me, but if not... "Just make sure you bring me the gun."

After she left I waited there alone in the dark all day. But not completely alone, for I fancied that I could feel the shadow man's presence, feel him connected to the soles of my feet, his will lurking in some murky recess of my mind. I tried to sleep but regrets, self-recriminations and concerns for Sreevani swam around my head making any form of respite impossible.

I got to my feet and paced back and forth across the small room, waiting for Sreevani to return. I could not stand it: the dark, the solitude, the worry. Where was she? Why hadn't she returned? What was keeping her? She had been gone for hours. What if she had been caught trying to break into Major Carpenter's bungalow? She might be in prison...or worse. What if she was dead?

If she wasn't back by nightfall, I decided, I would have to make my own way back to the temple. It would be difficult without the men to accompany me and put out the lights, but I couldn't just stay there in the dark. I felt helpless and guilty. If Sreevani was in trouble with the British she would need my help. All of this was my fault, a consequence of my actions. I had to do something.

I was pretty sure I could find the temple on my own, but I would have to stay in the shadows, detour where necessary to avoid the lights. I would need every bit of strength and resolve I could muster. But as we used to say in schoolboy Latin, *extremis malis extrema remedia*: desperate times call for desperate measures.

So, by the time I judged that night had well and truly come, and Sreevani still had not returned, I determined I would go to the temple to find her. And if that proved fruitless, go to the bungalow to get my caplock and put an end to it. I grabbed the calico bag containing my notebook, pencils—and the Black Diamond—and slung it over my shoulder.

Straight away, I was hit by a powerful urge to grasp the gem, stronger and more compelling than ever before. My stomach heaved. I felt like vomiting. My surroundings began to swim. I gritted my teeth and clenched my fists. If I passed out would the shadow man overwhelm me? I had to stay conscious. With my head pounding, I made my way out into the night, dashed across the street and threw myself into a narrow, dark alley. I collapsed in the shadows, my chest heaving and my breath coming in painful gasps.

Nearby, goats were bleating. A dog barked. Pungent, spicy cooking smells floated on the night air. I pushed my face into the ground and tasted dust.

Eventually I regained my self-control, readied myself, and moved off into the night shadows, careful to avoid not only the patches of lamplight but also the silvery light of the moon. By the time I reached the temple, I was soaked with sweat and out of breath, exhausted by the ordeal of resisting the will of the *Tcho-Tcho* shaman.

Thus far, I had avoided looking down, avoided the sight of the shadow. Afraid that seeing it might have some power over me. But now I chanced a fleeting look in the half light of the *ghats. It* waited for me, leered at me.

When I stumbled inside the temple, I heard Sreevani shriek my name, and saw her through blurred vision rushing towards me. Then I heard Shankar order the lamps to be dimmed. The next thing I knew he was by my side, taking my weight and helping me to the curtained alcove where I once again slumped into the cushions and lay there panting until my strength began to return.

"Did you get my gun?" I asked Sreevani.

She spoke to the priest in urgent Hindi. After a brief exchange, she slipped out through the curtain, leaving Shankar alone with me in the dark alcove.

The priest grabbed my shoulders. "If you kill yourself, you will set free the *Tcho-Tcho* shaman's shadow. It will roam unfettered wherever there is light until it finds another host. Perhaps one not as adept as yourself at holding the shadow man at bay."

"I don't know how much longer I can resist it," I admitted. "Have you learnt anything that might help me?"

He sighed. "I learned that you will not easily be rid of the Black Diamond. It has certain properties and even if you were to somehow separate yourself from the stone, I believe it would turn up again, as you would say, like a bad penny."

Somehow that did not surprise me. "Anything else?"

"Not anything you would want to hear."

I took a breath and braced myself for more bad news. "Try me."

He sighed again. "I learned that if the way is opened for the Old One, it will possess not only Banaras, but when it has fed on the blood and souls of the good people of this city, it will spread out and ultimately devour all living things on Earth until it fills

200

the world with its Oneness."

I shook my head in disbelief. "There must be something we can do."

"The only thing we can do is keep you in the dark. The shadow cannot exist without light."

Does that mean I have to stay in the dark my whole life, I wondered?

"But the shadow is getting stronger all the time," I said. "I can feel it in my head even now, and it will be impossible for me to hide in the dark forever. Eventually, one way or another, there will be light and what then?"

"If that happens," the Hindoo priest said solemnly, "you will open a forbidden doorway and bring chaos and death to our world."

It felt like I had been punched in the gut. How could it be that I was the one person in all the world who could destroy everything? *Me*. Giles Freeman from Stoke-on-Trent. How could that be possible? A boy who grew up next to a river and used to fish with his dad for tadpoles. How could I be so monumentally important? How could I have made such a terrible blunder?

I sat in silence for a time, deep in thought. Then I came to a decision. "I created this situation by translating the texts. People have died because of my ill-advised blundering. I have that on my conscience. So it is up to me. It's my responsibility to solve the problem."

"You are not entirely responsible," Shankar said. "We have known of the mysterious temple of the Old One for generations, but made the mistake of assuming it was just another cult. Banaras is rife with them. They established themselves here in the hope this sacred city would lend their beliefs legitimacy. It was not until we learned from Sreevani that her sister had disappeared that we became suspicious. We made enquiries and learned that some other devotees and temple workers had disappeared, and we began to realise something was wrong. If we had taken action then…"

"But you didn't. So now it falls to me to act. I have an idea, but I need your help."

I explained my proposal. After a brief remonstration, he reluctantly agreed. After all, there was too much at stake; too many lives at risk. In the end, he could see the logic of my scheme.

He left the alcove. I heard him speaking with Sreevani in Hindi on the other side of the heavy drapery. Her voice became loud and shrill. She pushed through the curtain and threw her arms around my neck. Her body shuddered with emotion, her cheek wet with tears as she pressed her face against mine. Then she suddenly shoved me away, berating me in street Hindi, sobbing and pummelling my chest with her fists.

I recalled the first time she had done this and the gesture unexpectedly choked me up. She was punching me, but it was a token of her affection, her love for me.

Shankar prised Sreevani from me, speaking soft, calming words into her ear as he led her away. I felt a profound sense of loss and regret. I had been a stranger to her and yet she had risked herself body and soul to protect me, comfort and make love to me when most would have abandoned me to my doom.

I was left alone with my thoughts for a long time while Shankar made arrangements. Thinking about Sreevani and Rogers, and the horrific events that had got me to this point, I decided to write everything down, to leave a record as a warning for others. I took the notebook and a pencil from my bag, careful to avoid touching the Black Diamond, and began this account.

I thought it would be difficult to write in the dark, but by using my thumb as a gauge in the left-hand margin, I felt confident I could keep my lines of writing separate and legible.

Shankar came back sometime during the night.

"Giles, I brought your caplock pistol, some ammunition, the Sanskrit writings and your translation notes. I think that is everything."

I gave a humourless chuckle. "How were you able to pilfer them from Major Carpenter's bungalow?"

"That's not your concern. But rest assured, there was no trouble. There will be no recriminations. I suspect they will assume you have them, which would now be correct."

After that I did not see him again until what must have been the early hours of the morning. As I had instructed, he returned with a stonemason and a navvy hauling a cart loaded with masonry blocks.

Now, as I write the final page of this account, shivering in the dark, I can hear the scrape of the stonemason's trowel, the wet splat of mortar, and the tap-tap-tap as he works by touch to wedge the rough-hewn stone blocks into place. I must finish writing now and pass the notebook to Shankar who sits on the other side of the wall, overseeing the work that will separate us forever. For in the pitch black I can see the wall going up in my mind's eye, higher and higher until shortly it will stretch from floor to ceiling, a foot thick, sealing me off from Banaras and the world.

With that thought in mind I released a long sigh of relief and resignation, for here, surely, I will be safe from even the smallest glimmer of light. Ironic, I realise, that this primeval city where I am to be entombed once bore the Sanskrit name of Kashi, which translates as the City of Light. Save some sort of cataclysm, light will never again reach this space and the world will be safe from the ravages of the malevolent Elephant God, or whatever the creature is, because this place will not only be my tomb, it will also be the hiding place of the Black Diamond and the prison of the *Tcho-Tcho* shaman's shadow.

The last brick is almost in place. I will now pass the notebook to Shankar.

Giles Freeman (signed)
16th March 1843

The Black Diamond of the Elephant God — Afterword

I love India: the people, the culture, the food, the land, the history… I think I might have lived there in another life, if such a thing is possible. I first visited India in my early twenties and have been there numerous times since. And although each time has been a new experience, the sounds, tastes and smells are always familiar.

I was reading an obscure nineteenth century travel narrative titled *Travels in India* by Captain Leopold von Orlich—which I purchased in a lovely two-volume hardback edition from Asian Educational Services on the outskirts of Delhi—when I began to chew over an idea for a Cthulhu Mythos novelette. I ended up creating a kind of mash-up where my story and threads of von Orlich's non-fiction account are woven together to make something new.

I wrote much of the story in India. I finished the first draft on a houseboat cruising about the brackish lagoons and lakes of the Kerala backwaters in South India. But it was Varanasi that brought the story to life. The Cthulhu Mythos seems to sit well in the dusty back alleys of that city. According to Hindu legend, Varanasi is more than 5,000 years old and is believed to be the oldest continually inhabited city in the world.

'The Black Diamond of the Elephant God' is original to this collection.

Publication History

'Ma Rung' — *Dreaming Down-Under* (ed. Jack Dann & Janeen Webb), HarperCollins Australia, 1998. *Dreaming Down-Under* (ed. Jack Dann & Janeen Webb), TOR Books (USA) (hardcover), 2000.

'Two Tomorrow' — *Eidolon #3* (ed. Jeremy G. Byrne, Jonathan Strahan, et al), Spring 1990. *Beyond Fantasy & Science Fiction* (ed. David Riley), UK, June/July 1995. *100 Lightnings* (ed. Stephen Studach), Paroxysm Press, 2016.

'Greater Garbo' *Australian & NZ PC User* (ed. Geoff Ebbs), October 1992.

'In the Light of the Lamp' — *Terror Australis* (ed. Leigh Blackmore), Hodder & Stoughton, 1993. *The Cthulhu Cycle* (ed. Robert M Price), Chaosium, USA, 1996. *Le Cycle de Cthulhu* (ed. Robert M Price, translated by Eric Holweck), Oriflam, France, 1998. *La Saga de Cthulhu* (ed. Robert M Price, translated by Eric Holweck), La Factoria de Ideas, Spain, 2006.

'Logic Loop' — *Aphelion #5* (ed. Peter McNamara), Summer 86/87. *Worlds in Small* (ed. John Robert Colombo), Cacanadadada Books, 1992. *Grandes Minicuentos Fantasticos* (ed. Benito Arias Garcia) (Spanish translation), Alfaguara, 2004. *100 Lightnings* (ed. Stephen Studach), Paroxysm Press, 2016.

'Harold the Hero and the Talking Sword' (written in collaboration with Jack Dann, incorporating his story 'The Talking Sword', Copyright © 1998 by Jack Dann. All rights reserved by the author) — *And Then…* Volume 2 (ed. Ruth Wykes and Kylie Fox), Clan Destine Press, Australia, 2017 Copyright © 2017 by Jack Dann and Steven Paulsen.

'Fixed in Time' – original to this collection.

'The Place' — *Terror Australis #1* (ed. Leigh Blackmore, Christopher Sequeira and Bryce J. Stevens), April 1988.

'The Wine Cellar' – original to this collection.

'Pest Control' — *Cthulhu: Deep Down Under* (ed. Steve Proposch, Christopher Sequeira and Bryce J. Stevens), Horror Australis 2014.

'Old Wood' — *Terror Australis #2* (ed. Leigh Blackmore, Christopher Sequeira and Bryce J. Stevens), July 1990. *Strange Fruit* (ed. Paul Collins), Penguin Books, 1995.

'The Sorcerer's Looking Glass' — *Fantastic Worlds* (ed. Paul Collins), HarperCollins Australia, 1997

'Christmas Morning' — *Hell's Bells: Stories of Festive Fear* by members of the Australian Horror Writers Association (ed. the AHWA Committee), AHWA, 2016.

'The Black Diamond of the Elephant God' — original to this collection.